"YOU BOYS ARE UNDER ARREST."

Young Adam spoke the words with authority. "Are you coming?"

"No, we ain't . . boy," said Kennedy, his hand slowly moving to his hip. "Why don't you just pull out that hogleg, Sheriff," he taunted, "and we'll settle this right here."

"I'm afraid I can't do that, boys."

"Why not?" Mead asked. "You yella?"

"No. It's just that my friend had something else in mind."

Mead guffawed. "What friend?"

Behind him, the Gunsmith rested his pistol on the back of the man's skull and clicked the hammer back. "That would be me."

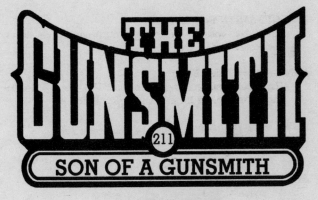

THE GUNSMITH

211

SON OF A GUNSMITH

J. R. ROBERTS

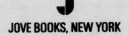

JOVE BOOKS, NEW YORK

SON OF A GUNSMITH

A Jove Book / published by arrangement with
the author

PRINTING HISTORY
Jove edition / August 1999

The Penguin Putnam Inc. World Wide Web site address is
http://www.penguinputnam.com

ISBN: 0-515-12557-1

A JOVE BOOK®
Jove Books are published by The Berkley Publishing Group,
a division of Penguin Putnam Inc.,
375 Hudson Street, New York, New York 10014.
JOVE and the "J" design
are trademarks belonging to Penguin Putnam Inc.

PRINTED IN THE UNITED STATES OF AMERICA

10 9 8 7 6 5 4 3 2 1

ONE

It was no great secret that Clint Adams, the Gunsmith, could often be found in the town of Labyrinth, Texas. However, it was unusual for anyone to try and find him there. Those who wanted to try their guns against his thought that riding into that town would be like cornering a bear in his own den. Newspapermen tried to approach him there, but they were not welcomed with open arms. The people of Labyrinth liked the idea that the Gunsmith was often among them, and for this reason they were protective of their favorite and most famous part-time citizen.

The woman who came looking for him that day was not a threat by any stretch of the imagination—unless carrying news to him was a threat.

And, of course, that would be for him to decide once he heard the news.

When the knock came at his door, Clint rolled over in bed and bumped into Shana, the long, lean, full-breasted beauty who was lying next to him.

"Huh?" she mumbled, lifting her head. She had lots of thick blond hair, which was wild and untamed in the morning. It danced around her head and fell over her forehead and eyes. All he could see was her jaw—a tad too square—

1

and her wide, full mouth—which more than made up for her jaw.

"It's the door," he said. "Go back to sleep."

She smiled, blew him a kiss, and put her head back down on the pillow.

Clint got out of bed and padded naked to the door.

"Who is it?"

"Mr. Adams, it's the desk clerk."

He frowned. He couldn't remember the clerk's name.

"What is it?"

"Uh, there's a woman waiting in the lobby to see you," the clerk said.

Clint opened the door a crack and looked at the man.

"What woman?"

"She wouldn't give me her name."

"Who is she, then?"

"She just said to tell you she was an old friend."

Clint frowned. He had lots of old friends. That didn't mean he was going to leave a warm bed and an even warmer blonde and go running to the lobby just because somebody *said* they were an old friend.

"What should I tell her?" the clerk asked.

"Tell her . . ."

"She seemed very anxious to see you."

"Is that so?"

"Said it was very important."

"Uh-huh."

"A matter of life and death."

"Hmmm."

"And she said to remind you about New Orleans at Thanksgiving."

"New Orleans . . . at Thanksgiving?"

"That's right. Does that mean something to you?"

"Yes, it does," Clint said. "Put the lady in the dining room and tell her I'll be down in about ten minutes. Okay . . . ?"

"Jerry," the clerk supplied.

"Right, Jerry."

"Okay," Jerry said.

"And thanks," Clint said. "I'll give you a little something when I have pants on."

"Sure thing, Mr. Adams," Jerry said, and Clint closed the door.

"What's this about New Orleans at Thanksgiving?" Shana Tweed asked.

Clint turned and saw the blonde looking at him. She had the prettiest eyes and the clearest, smoothest skin he'd ever seen.

"Is it some sort of code?"

"No," he said, looking around for his pants, "not a code."

"A signal from one of your other women?"

He smiled at her and said, "Right now you're all the woman I can handle."

"Then why are you putting on your pants?"

"To go downstairs and talk to somebody," Clint replied. "An old friend."

"A female old friend?"

"I have old friends of both sexes, Shana."

"Is this one pretty?"

He thought a moment, then said, "She was."

"What does she look like?"

"Dark, smaller than you."

"And when was this Thanksgiving in New Orleans?"

"Hmmm . . . if I'm remembering correctly, about twenty-three years ago."

"Twenty-three—*years*?"

He buttoned his shirt and looked around for his boots. "Uh-huh."

"Well," Shana said, "that's different."

Clint knew what she was thinking. How could a woman he knew twenty-three years ago be a threat to her now?

"Go down and see what your *old* friend wants," she

said, "and then come back up here and take care of your new friend."

To make her point more memorable, she tossed off the bedclothes and then stretched her long, lean, naked body.

"I'll be back," he promised, his mouth dry.

TWO

As he expected, the "old friend" waiting for him in the dining room was Olivia Broussard. She had been twenty years old when he had first met her. Now, twenty-three years later, she was even lovlier than ever. Gone was the vibrancy of youth, replaced with the quiet dignity of . . . well, experience. He knew he looked nothing like the twenty-odd-year-old that he'd been then, either. He doubted, however, that in his case the years as been as kind as they had obviously been to her.

"Olivia," he said, approaching the table.

"Clint," she said, standing quickly, nervously. "I would have known you anywhere. You look the same."

"You don't," he said.

"Well," she said defensively, "twenty-three years—"

"You look twenty-three years better," he said. "You're incredibly lovely."

"I . . ." He'd embarrassed her. "Please, sit down."

He waited until she sat first, then sat across from her. The waiter came over.

"Do you want anything?" Clint asked.

"I'm actually quite famished," she said. She ordered breakfast, and he was surprised to find that it was identical to what he usually had: steak and eggs. He ordered the same.

"When did you get to town?"

"Last night, on the late stage," she said. "I got a room at a hotel down the street. I didn't know where you were, then. I asked around this morning."

"You knew I was here?" he asked.

She reached across the table and put her hand over his.

"I came here to see you, Clint," she said. "I . . . I need help very badly."

He looked down at the hand that was covering his. It was her left, and there was a wedding ring on it.

"You're married," he said.

She pulled her hand away as if she'd been burned, and covered it with her right.

"Yes."

"To who?"

She hesitated, then said, "Troy Heathcote."

He smiled grimly. "The marriage your father wanted for you."

"Yes."

"Are you happy?"

"We've been married twenty-two years, Clint," she said. "What couple is happy after that much time together?"

"Were you ever happy?"

"Well . . ."

"He cheated, didn't he?" Clint asked. "Right from the beginning, probably right up to now—if he's still alive."

"He is."

"I thought some jealous husband might have killed him in a duel by now."

"Clint . . . I don't want to talk about Troy."

He took a deep breath, surprised that he could still hate Troy Heathcote and her father after all these years.

"All right," he said.

Breakfast came at that moment, and they both sat back and waited while the waiter set it on the table. He poured them each a cup of coffee and then withdrew.

"Any children?" he asked.

"Three," she said. "Two boys and a girl."

Clint smiled.

"How old is the girl?"

"Eighteen."

"I'll bet she's as beautiful as you were."

"The boys are twenty-two and twenty."

"Where are they?"

"Tracy—our daughter—lives with us in New Orleans. Henry, the younger boy, he's still there, too, but he has his own place."

"And the other boy?"

"That would be . . . Adam."

"Adam?"

She nodded. "I wanted to name him Clint, but Troy wouldn't hear of it."

"How did you slip Adam by him?"

She shrugged.

"He didn't seem to mind that so much."

Well, Clint thought, *nobody ever accused the young Troy Heathcote of being smart.* He always thought his father being rich would get him whatever he wanted—and it pretty much did.

"So where is Adam?"

"Well, right now he's in Caldwell, Kansas."

"Caldwell?"

"Yes."

"That used to be a pretty rough town."

"It still is, from what I hear."

"Well, what's he doing there?"

"As of two weeks ago," she said, "he was the sheriff."

"The sheriff? How old is he again?"

"Twenty-two."

"Does he have any experience being a law-enforcement officer?"

"No," she said. "He just wanted to go West, and that's where he ended up."

"And how did he become sheriff?"

"Nobody else wanted the job," she said. "Apparently there's some kind of gang using it as a headquarters."

"Why would this kid want to take on that kind of responsibility?"

"Well," she said, "it might have something to do with who his father is."

"You mean Troy?"

"No, Clint," she said, looking across the table at him. "I mean you."

THREE

"Say that again?"

"He's your son, Clint."

Clint sat back, his half-finished breakfast forgotten. Once before he'd run into this situation, where somebody claimed to be his son, but that had turned out to be false. This was different, though. There was not a young man claiming it, but the young man's mother *telling* him.

"How do you figure that?"

"After you left New Orleans," she began, "I found myself pregnant. That's why I agreed to marry Troy."

"And you told him it was his?"

"Yes."

"But . . . it was mine?"

"You're the only other man I was with."

Clint looked down at the table. All there was to drink was coffee, and he needed something stronger.

"You believe me, don't you?"

Clint didn't answer her directly. Instead, he asked, "Did you ever tell Adam this?"

"No," she said. "He believes that Troy is his father."

"Then what did you mean when you said his going West had something to do with who his father was?"

"I was talking about his blood," she replied. "It's yours,

9

and you told me all those years ago that you had the wan-
derlust. From what I hear you're still wandering around
most of the time.''

''That's true.''

''Well, he's the only one of my three children who felt
that way,'' she said. ''Henry and Tracy are content to stay
in New Orleans.''

''Olivia, why are you telling me this now?'' he asked.

''Because if you don't go there and help him, Clint,''
she said, ''he's going to get himself killed.''

''What can I do?''

''Keep him alive.''

''How?''

''Well, first, you can talk him out of being sheriff,'' she
said. ''If that doesn't work, then just stay there and help
him.''

''And how long do you think I'll be able to do that?''
he asked.

''As long as it takes to clean that gang out of Caldwell,''
she said. ''He said in a letter that he would only keep the
job that long.''

''So you want me to go there and help him and . . . what?
Tell him I'm his father?''

''No, no,'' she said. ''You can't do that. He'd hate us
both.''

''You want me to go help my . . . my son and not tell
him I'm his father?''

She pushed her half-eaten breakfast away.

''I know what I'm asking isn't fair, Clint,'' she said,
''but this is my son's life. I didn't know who else to turn
to.''

''What about Troy?''

''He's disowned Adam unless he comes home.''

''That stupid—''

''I know,'' Olivia said, ''but I couldn't talk him out of
it. He was determined to force Adam home that way.''

''And Adam won't go for it?''

"Adam wants to be on his own, Clint," she said. "He's very headstrong, very willful. He reminds me of . . . of you when you were that age."

Clint sat back in his chair. "I don't know what to tell you, Olivia."

"I know this is a lot to take in all at once," she said. "Why don't you take some time to think it over?"

"According to you," he said, "the boy doesn't have time for me to do that."

"It's only been two weeks," she pointed out. "In his letter, he said it would take time for people to take him seriously. Mightn't it be possible that this gang won't think him a threat right away?"

"Yes, it is possible," Clint agreed, "but if he's anything like me when I was that age. . . . Can he handle a gun, Olivia?"

"Very well," she said. "It seemed to come to him very naturally."

That could have been a coincidence, the boy's ability with a gun coming to him that way, Clint told himself.

"What will you do, Clint?"

"You're asking me to go there and help him."

"Yes."

"Then that's what I'll do."

"Because he's your son?"

"Because you're my friend," Clint said, "and I'd do the same for any friend."

"Then you don't accept him as your son?"

"I can't do that right now, Olivia," he said. "I—I've got to see the boy, first. Talk to him."

"But you'll help him anyway?"

"I'll offer him my help," Clint said, "but you've got to understand something."

"What's that?"

"He might not want it."

"Well, then, you'll just have to force it on him."

"I can't—"

"He'll know who you are, Clint," Olivia said. "He'll recognize your name. You're a legend. Why would he refuse your help?"

Because, Clint thought, *if he's anything like me when I was that age, he just might be that stubborn.*

FOUR

Instead of going back upstairs to Shana, Clint left the hotel and walked to Rick's Place, his friend Rick Hartman's saloon and gambling parlor. He knew Rick would be having his breakfast.

"Have some?" Rick asked after letting Clint in.

"No, but I'll have some coffee."

"What a surprise," Rick said. "You drink more coffee than any three men I know."

"Actually," Clint said, "I could use a beer."

"This early?"

"I got some interesting news this morning."

"What kind of news?"

"It seems I may be a father."

"Right," Rick said, "and what young gunny is claiming you as his father now?"

"It's not a kid, it's the kid's mother."

"Somebody you know?"

"Somebody I knew twenty-three years ago."

"I'm almost done with my breakfast anyway," Rick said. "Come up to the bar with me and I'll join you in a whiskey."

"Just a beer will do for me."

"Okay," his friend said, and drew them each a beer. After

13

they had both taken a healthy swallow, Rick said, "Tell me about it."

"So what are you going to do?" Rick asked, then held up his hand. "Wait. I'll tell you what you're going to do. You're going to Caldwell, to help this kid sheriff out, right?"

"Right."

"And why is this? Because you believe he's your son?"

"Because his mother is a friend of mine and asked for my help," Clint said.

"And that's the only reason?"

"Of course it's not the only reason," Clint replied. "I've got to take a look at this kid, Rick. I've got to talk to him and see what he's like. Wouldn't you do the same thing?"

His friend stared at him for a few moments, then said, "I have."

"What?"

"It was a few years back," he said. "A woman came to town claiming I was the father of her son."

"And?"

"I went to meet him, to get to know him. I even got to like him."

"And?"

"And as it turned out, he wasn't mine. Decent kid, though."

"And what happened?"

"Well . . . they still didn't know who his real father was, so I kind of, uh, send money once in a while."

"You're helping out."

"Well, yeah, helping out."

"Even though you know he's not yours."

"Well . . . he could have been. I mean, I did know his mother and . . . well, he might have been."

"You never told me this?"

"I never told anyone."

"So why now?"

"I don't know," Rick said. "Maybe just to help you make a decision."

"Well, I've already made a decision," he said. "I'll leave for Caldwell in the morning."

"Okay," Rick said, "I'll use the rest of today to try to find out what's going on in that town."

"Thanks."

"Come back by tonight and I might have some information. What are you going to do in the meantime?"

"Well, I've got a lady waiting for me in my hotel room," he said. "I think I'm going to have to soothe some ruffled blond feathers."

"Shana?"

Clint nodded.

"Helluva woman, Clint."

"I know it."

"She packs them in here for me every night. I've never seen her leave with a man other than you, but they don't seem to mind that. As long as she's here, every man has the illusion that one night—when you're not in town—she might."

"I wish them luck," Clint said. He finished the beer and pushed the empty mug away. "Thanks for talking to me."

"Sure."

"And thanks for the story—even if it's not true."

The other man looked at him for a few moments, then grinned. "How did you know it wasn't true?"

"Because I know you, Rick," Clint said. "You'd never have been able to keep something like that from me."

"Never?"

"Never," Clint said. "Not on a bet. I'll see you later."

FIVE

Clint wanted to talk to Shana, but when he got back to his room she wasn't there. Obviously, he was going to have some explaining to do to her later, but that was when he'd worry about it—later. At the moment he had to decide how he felt about possibly being a father.

Clint had never regretted that he had not married. He had come close once, but the woman had been killed. Since then his life just never seemed to have room in it for a wife. He simply liked moving around much too much for that.

His relationship with Olivia had been intense but brief, and he didn't know how he felt about the possibility that it had resulted in the birth of a son. If it was true, should he be angry that he'd never been told? Or happy to find out about it now? Did he want to be a father? It had never been a burning desire of his.

He decided there was no way he could decide how he felt about this in one night. One thing was for sure. He was going to have to meet the boy, and that meant going to Caldwell, Kansas—and while he was there he might as well do what he could to keep the boy alive.

• • •

Later that evening he went back to Rick's Place to kill two birds with one stone. He wanted to see what Rick had found out about the situation in Caldwell, and he had to talk to Shana and explain what had happened that morning.

When he entered, he asked the bartender where Rick was.

"He's in his office."

"And Shana?"

"She ain't come down yet."

Clint thanked him and walked back to Rick's office. He knocked on the door and entered.

"There you are," Rick said, from behind his desk. "I've been waiting for you."

"You've got some information?"

"Have I," Rick said. "Apparently, the McGovern Gang has moved into Caldwell."

"McGovern," Clint repeated. "I know that name."

"You should," Rick said. "They're wanted in Texas, Oklahoma, Missouri, and three more states for robbery and murder."

"But not in Kansas?"

"Not in Kansas, as far as I know."

Clint whistled soundlessly. "How many of them?"

"Half a dozen or so, from what I can find out," Rick said. "It sounds like young Junior has his work cut out for him."

Clint frowned.

"How are you feelin' about bein' a dad?" his friend asked.

"I'm not sure," Clint said. "It's not something I can just decide."

"Maybe it's something you're just supposed to feel?" Rick suggested.

"Maybe, but I don't."

"So you're going?"

"I have to," Clint said. "I have to see the boy and do what I can to help him."

"No matter whose son he is?"

"It doesn't matter who his father is, Rick," Clint said. "His mother is the one I'm doing this for."

"And if you're not his father, who is?"

"Her husband."

"Do you know him, too?"

"I did, twenty-three years ago. He was a spoiled brat then, from a wealthy New Orleans family."

"Which one?"

"Heathcote."

Now Rick whistled.

"You know the name?" Clint asked, although he realized he shouldn't have been surprised.

"I know it very well," Rick said. "They have holdings throughout Louisiana, not just in New Orleans."

"Holdings?"

"They're big in shipping."

"Shipping merchandise?"

"Building ships."

"Oh. I thought that was an East Coast industry."

"It is," Rick said. "They have offices in Pittsburgh, Philadelphia, Boston, and New York."

"They've expanded quite a bit over the years, then," Clint said.

"Which Heathcote is her husband?"

"That's right," Clint said, reminding himself, "there was more than one son."

"Three, if memory serves."

"She's married to Troy."

"The youngest son," Rick said. "The others are Remy and . . ."

"Charles," Clint said. "Charlie Heathcote. God, I haven't thought about him in years."

"Friends?"

"We were," Clint said, "and we were friendly rivals for Olivia."

"But she married Troy."

"Her father wanted her to marry one of the boys," Clint said. "Their father offered Troy."

"How did Charlie feel about that?"

"He wasn't happy."

"Well, apparently he wasn't so unhappy that he left the family business. He's in charge of their Boston operation."

"And Remy?"

"He's still in New Orleans, I think," Rick said. "This is from memory, now, but I could be wrong."

"You?"

"Want me to find out more?"

"Why not?" Clint asked. "I might as well know as much as I can."

"If you're leaving tomorrow, I might not have it by then."

"You can send it to me by wire," Clint said, opening the door, "in Caldwell."

"Where are you off to now?"

"I've got to talk with Shana," Clint said, "make sure she understands what's going on."

"She won't be happy that you're leaving."

"Can't be helped," Clint said. "Hopefully I can make her see that."

"She's a smart girl," Rick said. "Explain it right and she will see it."

"I'll do my best," Clint said, and left his friend's office.

SIX

When Clint came out of Rick Hartman's office, Shana was coming down the stairs from the second floor. She had the attention of every man in the place. Her long blond hair was perfectly piled atop her head now, revealing her long, graceful neck. Her shoulders were pale, as were the two perfect breasts that were barely contained by the blue gown she was wearing. Beneath the gown were, he knew, two perfectly formed long legs.

When she reached the main floor several men tried to attract her attention but she ignored them and strode across the room to Clint.

"I waited," she said.

"Not long enough," he said.

"I knew you'd say that. How was she?"

"Lovely, and in trouble."

"What kind of trouble?"

"Kid trouble," he said. "She has a son who thinks he's tough enough to be the sheriff of a tough town."

"Is he?"

"I don't know."

"But you're going to find out, right?"

"Right."

"When are you leaving?"

"In the morning."

"Well," she said, "that leaves us tonight."

"If you're not too mad at me."

"I'm mad at you," she said, "but not enough to miss tonight."

"There's one other thing, Shana."

"What?"

"There's a possibility he may be mine."

She frowned. "Your what?"

"My son."

"A possibility?"

"Yes."

"You don't know?"

"No."

"And she doesn't know?"

"She says he is."

"Ah . . ."

"What's that mean?"

"Just 'ah . . .' "

"So you understand why I have to go?"

"Of course," she said, and then added, "not that I have to, though."

"What?"

"You owe me an explanation for leaving me alone this morning," she said, "that's all. You don't owe me an explanation about anything else."

"Oh," he said. "All right, but I *wanted* to tell you."

She smiled, touched his arm and said, "That's good. I'll see you later and you can tell me more."

"What more is there to tell?"

"You can tell me how you feel about the situation," she said.

"I don't know how I feel."

"Well, maybe we can figure it out together."

"Yes, maybe . . . thank you, Shana."

Her smile broadened. "What are friends for? I have to go to work. See you later."

He watched as she walked across the floor and stopped at a table filled with men. They all started talking to her at one time, and he heard her laughter float across the room. Every man in the place wished she were laughing with him—or even at him.

He knew she'd be in bed with him tonight, so he walked proudly to the door and left.

SEVEN

Clint walked to Olivia's hotel, ascended the steps to the second floor, and knocked on her door. When she opened it, an expectant look in her eyes, she suddenly became flustered as she saw it was him.

"Clint!"

"Can we talk?"

"Oh . . . well, not here . . ."

"I'll wait in the lobby," he said. "The dining room is still open. I'll buy you a cup of coffee."

"All right. I, uh, I'll be right down."

Clint nodded, turned, and went back down to the lobby. Why had she been so nervous? Did she think he'd want to take up where they had left off twenty-three years ago? Even though she was a desirable woman, they weren't the same people now that they had been then. He'd never have expected her to simply invite him into her room and jump in bed with him, nor did he want that. He had more important things to discuss with her than sex.

He went into the dining room to wait for her.

By the time she arrived he had a pot of coffee and two cups on the table.

"I'm sorry," she said, seating herself across from him,

"you caught me by surprise. I thought we were going to talk tomorrow."

"I can't talk tomorrow," he said, filling her cup. "I'll be leaving in the morning."

"You mean . . ."

"Yes," he said, "I'm going to Caldwell."

She closed her eyes for a moment, looked as if she was holding her breath, and then released a sigh.

"Thank you, Clint!"

"Before I leave," he said, "we need to talk a bit about . . . about Adam."

"What about him?"

"Well, for one thing, how do you want me to do this?" Clint asked.

"What do you mean?"

"Do you want to send him a telegram and tell him I'm coming to help him?"

"Oh, no!" she exclaimed. "He'd never accept your help if he thought I had sent you."

"Then I'll just have to ride into town cold," he said, "find some way to meet him and offer my help—or get him to ask for it."

"He's too proud to ask for it," she said.

"I'll find a way, then," he promised. "Does his father . . . does Troy know what's going on?"

"What do you mean, exactly, by 'going on'?" she asked.

"I mean, does he know that his son is the sheriff of Caldwell, Kansas? Does he know that you came here looking for my help?"

"He doesn't care what Adam is doing," she said. "He just wants him to come back. And no—good Lord, no— he doesn't know that I came to see you. He would have simply forbade that."

"And when he forbids something—" Clint started to ask, but he stopped. "Troy's father isn't still alive, is he?"

"No, he died years ago."

"And your father?"

"He also died."

"And your mother?"

"She died soon after Father," she said. "A broken heart, I think."

"I liked your mother," he said. "I'm sorry."

"She liked you, too."

They sat silently for a moment, awkwardly, before he spoke again.

"What will you do now? Once I leave?"

"I'll go home," she said. "I'll wait there to hear from you or from Adam. Hopefully, when I do hear, it won't be bad news."

"Does he have any friends in Caldwell?"

"I don't know," she said. "I don't think so. He's never mentioned any."

"Do you know anything about the men he's going up against?"

"No," she said, "he didn't tell me. Do you know something?"

"I know it's the McGovern Gang, run by a man named Frank McGovern."

"How . . . how many of them are there?"

"I've heard six," he said. "I'll know better when I get there."

"Will you . . . send me a telegram—"

"Olivia," he interrupted, "I won't send anything until it's all over. I think it's better that way."

"Well, all right," she said. "Maybe . . . maybe Adam will write. . . ."

"Maybe."

Another awkward silence passed. Clint had never been this uneasy with a former lover before, but then none of them had come to him and told him he had a son.

"What time will you be leaving?" she asked finally.

"Early," he said. "First light."

"Then . . . I should say good-bye now."

"Yes."

"And thank you."

"Don't thank me yet, Olivia," Clint warned as they both stood up, she to leave and he because *she* was.

"Oh, yes," she said. "You don't have to do this, you know."

"I know."

She studied him for a moment, then started to put her hand out, but drew it back.

"I'll . . . wait to hear from you."

"I'll do what I can for the boy, Olivia."

"I know you will."

As she turned to leave, he said, "Oh, I forgot. Can you give me a description of him?"

She turned back, smiled, and said, "Oh, I think you'll know him when you see him."

EIGHT

Clint felt lucky not only to know Shana Tweed, but to have her share his bed. She was not a kid. In fact, she was a little old for the job she was doing—in her mid- to late thirties—but her extraordinary beauty seemed timeless. Much like Olivia Heathcote, she seemed to be lovlier *because* of her age.

Clint waited for Shana outside Rick's Place, as he had the last eight or nine nights, and they went to his hotel room. Wordlessly, they had undressed each other. He enjoyed undressing her, bringing her naked body into view little by little. He would immediately grow rock hard when her breasts would burst forth from her gown. They were lovely, pale, firm, tipped with pink; there was the same odd strawberry mark just above the aureole of each nipple.

He gathered her breasts into his hands and kissed them, enjoying the feel of her smooth flesh against his lips, and beneath his tongue. He spent a long time on her breasts, time she seemed to appreciate very much. She moaned and sighed and held his head and gasped when his lips finally closed over first one nipple, then the other, pulling on them, sucking them, then nipping them until they were hard nubs.

Once they were naked they tumbled into bed together. She used her mouth on his body, bringing it alive, sliding

29

down until she was between his legs, making love to his cock. She held it, cooed to it, ran her finger up and down the smooth underside, finding that very sensitive spot just below the spongy head. When she found it she leaned forward and wet it with her tongue, then circled the head of his cock before engulfing him, taking him deep into her mouth, lovingly running the lips of her smooth, sensuous mouth over him, sliding him in and out, wetting him thoroughly. She sucked him until he was lifting his butt off the bed, moaning and reaching for her, and then she mounted him and hurriedly stuffed him inside of her. She tossed her head back, her hair hanging long and free, and he watched her breasts sway and bounce as she rode him, tugging on him with her insides, dragging his orgasm from him just moments before her own body was racked with pleasure. . . .

He talked with her about what he was going to do, and she listened. He appreciated the fact that when she asked questions they were about Adam, and not about Olivia.

"What will you do?" she asked.

"When?"

"When you see him. What will you do if you take one look at him and know he's yours?"

He was silent for a moment, then said, "I really don't know. I mean, I'll be there to keep him alive, and that's what I'll do, but . . ." His voice trailed off helplessly.

"But will you tell him?" she asked.

"I don't know, Shana. I guess before I mentioned it to him I'd have to be sure of it myself."

"And what would it take for that to happen?"

"I . . . don't know."

She propped herself up on an elbow and looked down at him.

"I haven't known you long, Clint, but I've never known you to be this indecisive about anything."

"This is . . . intensely personal. I don't know when I've

had to deal with anything this personal. I mean . . . a son."

"Have you ever thought about having children?"

"Not for a very long time."

"You've known a lot of women," she said. "None have ever come forth before with something like this?"

"No," he said. "There was a young man once who was telling people he was my son. . . ."

"What happened?"

Clint shrugged and said, "He wasn't."

"How did you deal with it then?"

"I never believed it," he said. "It was totally different from this."

She lay back down, her head on his shoulder. He put his arm around her.

"I wish I could help you," she said.

"You can't," he said. "This is my problem, something I have to handle alone."

"Well," she said, sliding her hand down over his belly, "you're leaving early in the morning, so we really shouldn't be wasting time talking, should we?"

Later, as Shana lay beside him, sleeping deeply, he thought about what she had said. He had known many women over the years. What if there were others he had left with child? What if he had other sons and daughters out there that he didn't know about?

He fell asleep, finally, and dreamed about dozens of children, all ages, chasing him and calling him Poppa.

NINE

Clint woke at first light, dressed, and then stared down at Shana's sleeping form. She was on her belly, the sheet down around her waist. He stared at the beautiful line of her back, tracing it with his eyes until it disappeared between her perfect buttocks, the tops of which just peeked out from the sheet. He would have liked nothing better than to get undressed and crawl right back into bed with her, snuggle up warm next to her, inhale the scent of her body, of their sex . . . but he couldn't. He leaned over, lifted the sheet and kissed each perfect buttock without waking her, and then left the room.

When he got to the livery to saddle Duke, he was surprised to find Rick Hartman there waiting for him, sitting on a barrel.

"Coming with me?" he asked.

"Not likely," Rick said, "but I thought you might like some coffee before you left." He motioned to the ground next to him, to a tray with a coffeepot and two cups.

"I could, thanks."

Rick poured them each a cup and handed one to Clint.

"I found out some things about the McGoverns."

Clint sat next to him on another barrel and said, "I'm listening."

"Frank's the leader."

"I knew that."

"He's got a brother, Virgil," Rick continued. "The way I hear it, he's a troublemaker, not exactly right in the head."

"Younger brother?"

"Yeah," Rick said, then frowned. "Why's that matter?"

"It's been my experience," Clint said, "that older brothers are very protective of younger brothers. Probably more so in a situation like this. What else have you got?"

"The last time the gang did a job was a train in Missouri. There were eight of them, and the train had a full complement of guards on it."

"Did they pull the job off?"

"No," Rick said. "The guards fought them off, even killed two of them, and the gang didn't get a dime."

"That'd make them testy."

"The guards think they might have wounded one or two others."

"How long ago was that?"

"A month."

"So they probably holed up in Caldwell, licking their wounds."

"The way I hear it," Rick said, "they like the town, made it their own. They take what they want and they don't pay."

"They might never leave."

"That's what I was thinking."

"Unless they're driven out," Clint said.

"That might be what the young man has in mind."

Clint drained his cup and put it back on the tray.

"Thanks for the coffee. Got any more information for me?"

"No, just some advice."

"Which is?"

"Don't lose sight of who you are," Rick said.

"What's that mean?"

"I just mean don't start thinking of yourself as a daddy, and the boy as your son—not when you've got the Mc-Govern gang to deal with. The boy's the sheriff and you're the Gunsmith—I know you don't like that name, but that's who you are. You want to play father and son, do it after the gang has been taken care of."

Clint thought for a moment, then nodded and said, "That is good advice. Thanks."

He got up, went inside, and saddled Duke. In the stall next to the big gelding was a canvas sack. He looked inside and saw that it was full of supplies. A going-away present from Rick Hartman, no doubt. He tied the sack to his saddle horn, mounted, and rode outside; Rick was still sitting there.

"Thanks for the supplies," Clint said.

"Had a feeling you might not have thought of it."

"You were right; I didn't."

Rick walked over.

"That's what I mean," he said. "You're already pre-occupied over this. Clear your head before you ride into Caldwell, Clint, or instead of keeping that boy alive you'll die right alongside of him."

"I'll keep that in mind."

"You do that—oh, and keep me informed, huh? Let me know what's going on? I'm, uh, interested."

"You want to know if the boy is my son?"

"Damn right I do."

Clint smiled.

"You're a good friend, Rick."

"I try."

"As soon as I know whether or not he's mine," Clint said, "you'll be the first to know."

"That's all I'm asking," Rick said, and then added, "Oh, yeah, and stay alive."

"I'll make that my priority."

He waved, turned Duke, and rode out of Labyrinth.

TEN

Frank McGovern watched his younger brother, Virgil, eat. Virgil performed this simple task with the utmost of concentration, something that had fascinated Frank since they were children. There wasn't much else Virgil was good for because of a terribly short attention span, but when it came to eating, he managed to concentrate until the last morsel of food was gone.

And then he asked, "You gonna eat yours, Frank?"

"Naw, Virg," Frank said, pushing his half-finished plate across the table, "I'm done. You go ahead and finish it."

As he smoked a cigarette, Frank watched Virgil polish off the other half of his steak and marveled at how much his brother could eat and still stay rail thin. He wondered if the fact that his brother could never stand still had anything to do with it.

"I finished, Frank," Virgil announced.

"I see that, Virg."

Virgil sat back.

"You said I could have one after dinner."

Frank finished his cigarette, dropped the butt to the floor, and crushed it out with the toe of his boot.

37

"Did I?"

"Yeah, you did," Virgil said, "I remember."

That was another thing. Virgil had a terrible memory, but he could remember being promised a candy if he finished his dinner.

"Lemon or cherry?" Frank asked.

Virgil thought a moment, then said, "Lemon."

Frank produced the candy stick and gave it to Virgil, who immediately popped it into his mouth and began to suck noisily.

"Why don't you go outside and finish that, Virg?" Frank suggested.

"Sure, Frank."

Virgil pushed his chair back so hard it almost fell over and ran outside.

The woman at the table stared at Frank.

"Why do you make me sit here and watch him eat?" she demanded.

"He's my brother."

"That's right," she said, "he's your brother, not mine." She looked around the small restaurant to see if people were still watching them. "Why can't he eat by himself?"

"He's my brother," Frank repeated. "If you want to be with me you'll eat with him."

Jesus, Mandy Parker thought, *at least he doesn't make me* sleep *with that idiot.* That would be too much to bear. Mandy didn't know how the whores could stand sleeping with an idiot.

"Finish your dinner."

Actually, she *could* finish hers now that Virgil was gone. He so disgusted her that she could never eat when he was around.

"All right."

Frank McGovern watched Mandy Parker eat. It gave him no pleasure at all. The only pleasure he got from her was sticking his dick into her, and she allowed him to stick it anyplace he wanted, that was how badly she wanted to stay with him. So badly that she'd put up with Virgil's eating habits. Frank McGovern knew that Mandy was in love with him, but he also knew that, pretty soon, he was going to grow tired of sticking it in her, no matter *where* she let him put it, and he was going to have to find himself another woman. In fact, if she continued to complain about Virgil, that might come sooner than later.

Frank had promised his mother on her deathbed that he'd watch out for his brother. She needn't have made him promise, though, because he would have done it anyway. Virgil was the only person in the world Frank McGovern loved. For that reason his women would have to put up with him, and so would the men who worked for him. They all knew it, too. If you wanted to love Frank, or work for him, you had to deal with Virgil.

Some of the men didn't seem to mind. Sam Hawkins, for example, was very patient with Virgil, like an adult with a child. Larry Doby actually seemed to like Virgil. The others just put up with him, but that was okay. Hawkins and Doby had been with Frank the longest; they were the ones he trusted and counted on.

Virgil was twenty-four, and Frank was ten years older. Giving birth to Virgil had put a great strain on their mother. She'd recovered, but had never been the same, and when Virgil was ten she finally died. By then their father was already two years in the ground, so after they buried their mother Frank sold the house and the land, and he and Virgil took to the trail.

Frank formed his gang and when they went on jobs he would leave Virgil with whatever woman he happened to be keeping company with. He started taking Virgil on jobs with him when the boy turned sixteen. Virgil was able to do simple tasks, like collecting wood for the fire and feeding the horses. He couldn't do much else, though; and although he begged to be allowed to carry a gun, Frank wouldn't let him. No telling what he'd do with a gun, maybe even shoot himself by accident.

• • •

Mandy finished her dinner and pushed her plate away. She was relieved that with Virgil gone the other people in the restaurant had stopped watching them. Even though the townspeople were afraid of Frank they found Virgil funny and fascinating. They laughed at him behind his back, and sometimes to his face if he was alone. It was the only way they had of getting back at Frank and his gang.

Except now they had a sheriff.

"What are you gonna do about that sheriff?" she asked Frank.

"He's just a kid."

"A kid who's not afraid of you," she said. "A kid who's wearing a gun and a badge."

"Mandy," Frank said, "the sheriff is my business, and you're supposed to keep your nose out of my business, right?"

"Fine," she said, "I'll keep my nose out of your business. Can I go back to the hotel now?"

"Sure, go ahead."

She started to get up, then stopped and put her hand on his.

"Will you be coming soon, honey?" She got all tingly inside when she thought about Frank being in bed with her. He was so good she could stand anything—even watching Virgil eat.

"I'll be along," he said, sliding his hand out from under hers, "later. Just be ready for me."

"Oh, I will, honey," she said seductively. "You know I will."

Frank watched her walk out of the restaurant. The other men in the place did, too. She was a big, full-bodied blonde who would probably start to get fat when she hit thirty, which wouldn't be for a few years yet. Men liked to watch her walk, and in bed she was uninhibited and knew a hundred ways to give a man pleasure with her body.

Maybe he'd keep her around a little longer.

She was right about one thing, though. If he ignored that young sheriff, the little shit might just up and bite him on the ass. He was going to have to take care of him eventually.

ELEVEN

Clint rode into Caldwell and found it unchanged to the naked eye. He'd been there many times before, during times when men of great fame were around. Men like Wyatt Earp, Bat Masterson, and Bill Tilghman had all put in their time in Caldwell. Oh, yes, and Clint Adams . . .

But none of those men were around now, or the McGovern gang would not be running roughshod over the town. The safety of the town was now in the hands of an inexperienced twenty-two-year-old who might or might not be his son.

It was quiet as he rode down the main street. It was not yet noon, certainly late enough in the day for people to be doing business. Was this a result of the McGovern Gang's presence? No one on the streets, businesses keeping their doors closed?

He rode to the far end of town, then turned right and headed for the livery. When he got there he was greeted by a liveryman in his sixties, who was shaking his head as Clint dismounted.

"You don't want to do that, mister," the man said to him.

"Do what, old-timer?"

"Stop here."

"Why not?"

"It's become a bad place."

"How bad could it be?"

"You heard tell of the McGovern Gang?"

"Some," Clint said. "Heard they were wanted in a few states, if that's what you mean."

"Well, they ain't wanted in Kansas, which is why they're holed up here."

"The McGovern Gang is here?" Clint feigned surprise.

"Done took over the whole town. Looked pretty quiet to you riding in, didn't it?"

"I noticed that," Clint said. "I thought maybe there was a funeral, and most of the town was at church, or up on Boot Hill."

"No funeral," the man said, "but if them McGoverns stay any longer they could turn this place into a ghost town."

"What about the law?"

The man made a face.

"You got a sheriff, don't you?"

"Some young feller who went and made himself sheriff," the man said.

"Is that legal?"

"Well, that ain't what I meant to say," the older man replied. "What I meant was nobody else wanted the job so he stepped up and the mayor pinned a badge on him."

"So how's he been doing against the gang?"

"Ain't done nothin', yet," the man said. "He's still tryin' to get the town to take him serious, let alone them gang members."

"Well, you know what?" Clint said. "Sounds like an interesting situation to me. Maybe I'll stay around a few days and watch."

The man shrugged his bony shoulders and accepted Duke's reins from Clint.

"Suit yourself," he said. "I was just tryin' to save you some trouble."

"Well, I appreciate that, old-timer, I really do," Clint said. "And I'll keep everything you said in mind."

"You do that," the man said.

"What do I owe you?"

"You can settle up when you leave," the man said, and then muttered beneath his breath, "if you're still alive . . . durn fool . . ."

Clint smiled, took his rifle and saddlebags, and walked to the Caldwell House Hotel to get himself a room and a bath.

If he was going to meet his son, he wanted to be clean when he did it.

TWELVE

Clint was anxious to meet the sheriff, and he had a perfect way to do it. He often stopped in to see the local law when he came to town, to announce both his arrival and his intention of staying out of trouble.

He was hungry and he wanted a beer, but when he left the hotel he intended to walk right over to the sheriff's office. As he stepped through the doorway, though, a voice stopped him.

"Just get to town?"

He turned his head and saw a man sitting in a wooden chair. He had a piece of wood in one hand and a knife in the other, but there were no wood shavings on the ground.

"That's right," Clint said. "What about it?"

"Just thought you should know," the man said, "this town is, like, occupied."

"Occupied?"

"Sure, like in the war. Remember? You Yankees came in and occupied southern towns."

"I don't hear a southern accent," Clint said.

The man grinned and said, "I lost it."

He was old enough to have been in the war, but probably as an enlisted man. His eyes didn't look like officer's eyes.

"Are you the greeter?" Clint asked.

"That's me, the greeter."

"What's your name?"

"Sam."

"Just Sam?"

"That's all you need to know."

"Well, Sam, suppose you tell me who's occupying the town?"

"Frank McGovern."

"Oh, yeah," Clint said, "I think the liveryman said something about that."

"You think?"

"I wasn't listening real good."

"The liveryman mentioned Frank McGovern and you wasn't listening very good?"

"That's what I said."

"You know who Frank McGovern is?"

"I think he's some kind of crook, isn't he? Robs church poor boxes and such?"

The man stiffened and stood up. He dropped the block of wood he was holding, but held onto the knife. He had a well-worn Colt on his right hip.

"You better watch what you say, mister," Sam said.

"Actually," Clint said, "I don't have anything else to say. This conversation is over."

He stepped into the street and started to walk away.

"Hey!"

He didn't answer.

"Hey, you! What's your name?"

"Check the hotel register," Clint called back, and kept walking. He didn't turn to look behind him.

When he got to the sheriff's office, he stopped outside the door, wondering if he was doing the right thing. Maybe he should wait for the sheriff to come to him. But maybe he wouldn't. Maybe he'd be so preoccupied with the McGovern Gang he wouldn't notice another stranger in town.

Clint knocked, and then entered. He was surprised at how

nervous he was, but after all, how often did he get to meet a grown son—if it *was* his son.

There was a young man sitting at the only desk in the room, and when he looked up at Clint they locked gazes for a few moments. If this was, indeed, his son, was there something passing between them? Some kind of recognition, maybe?

The boy looked younger than twenty-two. That was probably why there was some trouble getting the town to accept him as the local law. He was slender but not skinny, sort of like Clint. There was no telling how tall he was while he was seated, but as if he could read minds the kid stood up. He was tall, probably a shade under Clint's own six feet. He still had some growing to do, but he was a good-looking boy.

"Can I help you?" Sheriff Adam Heathcote asked.

"Um," Clint said, suddenly tongue-tied. "Um, yeah, you're the sheriff?"

"That's right. Sheriff Adam Heath."

He'd shortened his father's last name to "Heath." The father he knew, anyway. His voice was not deep, but it wasn't high, either. It fit him.

"Um, yes, well, Sheriff, I just got to town and thought I'd stop in and introduce myself."

"Why would you do that, sir?" he asked.

"Just common courtesy."

"Are you a lawman, then? Is this professional courtesy?"

"No," Clint said, "no, not exactly."

Heath frowned.

"Then I don't understand."

"My name is Clint Adams, Sheriff."

"Adams?"

"That's right."

It took a moment, but recognition seeped in and the boy's eyebrows shot up.

"*Clint* Adams?"

50   J. R. ROBERTS

"Yes."

"The *Gunsmith*?"

"That's right," Clint said. He stepped forward and extended his hand. "Nice to meet you, Sheriff."

THIRTEEN

The sheriff hesitated, then took Clint's hand and shook it.

"It's a pleasure to meet you, sir."

Clint swallowed and said, "It's nice to meet you, too."
He just managed to avoid adding, "son."

"Uh, well, I guess I should ask you how long you're
staying in town," Heath said. "I, uh, I'm pretty new to this
job. I've only had it a couple of weeks."

"I wondered," Clint said. "I, uh, thought you were kind
of young."

"Yes, well," Heath said, "the truth of the matter is, uh,
no one else wanted the job."

"Because of the McGoverns?"

"You heard about that?"

"The liveryman warned me," Clint said, "and then
some fella named Sam—"

"Hawkins," Heath said. "He's one of McGovern's
men."

"I figured," Clint said. "He sort of wanted to set me
straight on who was running things."

"Well, they *think* they're running things."

"You're going to stop them?"

"I'm going to try."

"How many deputies do you have?"

51

"None."

"Friends in town?"

"None."

Clint considered offering his help right then and there, but decided it wasn't the right time.

"Well," he said instead, "sounds like you've got your work cut out for you, Sheriff. I'll leave you to it."

He started to leave, then turned back.

"Oh, to answer your question," he said, "I'll probably only be in town two or three days."

"I see," Heath said. "All right."

Clint nodded, and started for the door again.

"Mr. Adams?"

Clint stopped. Maybe the boy was going to ask.

"Yes?"

"When McGovern finds out you're in town he might try to recruit you."

Clint smiled.

"I'm not much of a joiner, Sheriff," he said. "You don't have to worry about that."

"Good," Heath said, "good, because I've got enough to worry about as it is."

"Yes, you do," Clint said, and left the office.

He walked across the street, found a doorway, and stepped into it. He stood watching the door of the sheriff's office. Maybe he was hoping the boy would come looking for him to ask for his help, but no. The door remained closed. For all intents and purposes the boy still intended to go up against the McGovern Gang alone.

Clint had two choices, as he saw it. He could go back across the street and offer the young sheriff his help, or he could go and talk to Frank McGovern, see what the man had in mind.

Maybe he could talk some sense into McGovern.

Maybe he could talk him into moving on to another town.

And maybe he'd sprout wings and not need Duke to get around anymore.

He stepped out of the doorway.

When he got back to his hotel, Sam Hawkins wasn't out front anymore. There still weren't any wood shavings on the ground. He went inside and approached the desk.

"Can I help you, sir?" the young desk clerk asked.

"Can you tell me where to find Frank McGovern?" Clint asked.

Instantly, the clerk looked frightened.

"N-no, sir," he stammered, "I don't have anything to do with Mr. McGovern."

"I know you don't, son," Clint said. "I'm just asking if you know where he is."

"No, sir."

"Does he have a room in this hotel?"

"No, sir."

"Then where does he stay?"

"H-he took over the mayor's house, at the north end of town. Moved the mayor and his family out."

"So then where's the mayor and his family staying?" Clint asked.

"They have rooms here."

"What's the mayor's name?"

"Barnaby," the clerk said, "Mayor Tom Barnaby."

"And what room is he in?"

"Room Four," the clerk said. "He and his wife are in Four, his daughter is in Five."

"Okay," Clint said. "That wasn't so hard. Thank you."

"S-sure."

Clint started to turn, then stopped.

"One more thing."

"Yes, sir?"

"After I left earlier did a man come in and look at your register?"

"Y-yes, sir," the clerk said. "One of McGovern's men."

"Okay, thanks. Is the mayor in his room?"

"As far as I know."

Clint nodded and went up the stairs to the second floor.

FOURTEEN

Clint knocked on the door of Room Five and was surprised when it was opened by a pretty girl in her early twenties.

"Yes?" she asked. She had long brown hair, wide brown eyes, and a bee-stung mouth. Her body was slender, her skin pale and smooth.

"I'm sorry," he said. "I was looking for Mayor Barnaby."

"I'm his daughter, Gretchen," she said. "What do you want with my father?"

"I just want to talk to him."

Her look turned suspicious and she asked, "Are you one of McGovern's men? I don't recognize you."

"No, ma'am, I'm not with McGovern," he said. "I just got to town today."

"And you want to see my father? Why?"

"It's kind of complicated."

She folded her arms.

"I have time."

Suddenly, Clint realized his mistake: The mayor was in Four.

"I'll go next door and talk to your father," he said. "I have no objection if you come along and listen. That way I won't have to say it twice."

55

"My father's not in."

"I'll knock and find out."

"All right, wait," she said, holding out one hand. "I'll come with you."

She stepped into the hall and closed the door to her room.

"McGovern and his men took our house," she said, as they moved across the hall to her parents' room.

"So I've been told."

She knocked and a woman's quavery voice called out, "Who is it?"

"My mother," Gretchen explained to Clint. "She's been afraid ever since..." She didn't finish. "Mother, it's Gretchen."

The lock was turned, then the door opened and a woman appeared. She was in her fifties, an older, handsome rather than pretty version of Gretchen.

"Oh!" she said when she saw Clint. Her hand flashed to her throat.

"He says he's not one of McGovern's men," Gretchen said, taking her mother's other hand. "He just got to town today, and he wants to talk to Father."

"Your father is resting," the woman said.

"I'm awake," a man's voice said. "Let them come in, Louisa."

As Clint and Gretchen entered the room, he saw a large, barrel-chested man getting up from the bed. He was wearing a shirt, trousers, and a vest, but was in his stocking feet.

"Mayor Barnaby?" Clint asked.

"I guess you can call me that," Barnaby said. "I was mayor until McGovern and his men showed up. What can I do for you, sir?"

"Mayor, my name is Clint Adams—"

"Good God!" Barnaby exploded, surprising all three of the other people in the room. "Close that door, Gretchen!"

"Father, I don't—"

"Close the door, girl!" he said urgently, and his daughter obeyed.

"Father, what is it?" she asked.

"Our prayers have been answered," Barnaby said delightedly. "Do you know who this man is?"

"Well, no—"

"Clint Adams!"

"He said that—"

"The Gunsmith, girl," Barnaby said. "He's the Gunsmith . . . our savior!"

FIFTEEN

"Praise the Lord!" Louisa Barnaby said.

"Mr. Adams," Barnaby said, grabbing Clint's hand and pumping it energetically, "you don't know how happy I am to see you, sir."

"Mayor," Clint said, pulling his hand free, "before you go any further you better listen to what I have to say. I'm nobody's savior."

"We tried hiring gunmen," Barnaby said, "but none of them would take the job when they heard they had to go up against the McGovern Gang."

"I don't blame them."

"We finally had to hire a sheriff—just anyone! A young man stepped up and wanted the job and I . . . well, I gave it to him."

"Threw him to the wolves is more like it," Gretchen Barnaby said. "He's so brave and kind, and you gave him a badge and made him a target."

Gretchen was obviously angry with her father, and just as obviously had feelings for young Adam Heath.

"He's no lawman, Mr. Adams," she said, "and he's all alone. They're going to kill him, I know it."

"Not if Mr. Adams here takes over," Mayor Barnaby said.

"What?" Gretchen said.

"You didn't want young Heath to take the job," Barnaby said to his daughter, "so now he can give it up and we can have a real sheriff."

"You have no feelings at all, do you?" Gretchen said angrily. "If you take his badge away now it would crush him."

"Dear," Louisa said, "your father is only trying to do what's best."

"Then make Mr. Adams the deputy," she said. "Adam would accept that."

"Hello?" Clint said. "Does anyone want to ask Mr. Adams if he would accept that?"

"See?" Barnaby said to his daughter. "He wants to be sheriff, not deputy."

"I don't want to be sheriff *or* deputy," Clint said, loud enough so that they could all hear it.

"But . . . we'd pay you," Barnaby said.

"I didn't come here looking for a job, Mayor," Clint said.

"Well then, why *did* you come?"

"Well . . . I did want to talk about a job, but not for me. I want you to keep Ad—Heath on as sheriff."

"Why? He can't possibly handle this gang."

"Then why did you give him the job in the first place?" Clint asked.

"Because nobody else wanted it."

"That's no reason to give a man a job you know is going to get him killed."

"We *needed* a sheriff," Barnaby said, "and he was the only applicant. What was I supposed to do?"

"Well, you could have tried hiring a lawman from outside."

"I told you, we tried that—"

"No," Clint interrupted, "you tried hiring gunmen. You should have gone for a lawman."

"Lawman, gunman," Barnaby said, as if the terms were

interchangeable. "We need someone who can handle a gun, and you fit the bill better than anyone. Name your price."

"I don't have a price."

"Everyone has a price."

"Well, then," Clint said, "you couldn't afford me."

"I'm a desperate man, Adams," Barnaby said.

"You want your town back, Mayor?"

"Of course I do."

"And your house?"

"Well, yes . . ."

"You hired yourself a sheriff; you're going to have to stand by him."

"How do I do that?" Barnaby asked. "He's a boy, with no experience—"

"Get him a deputy," Clint said, "and show the towns-people you believe in him. Maybe they will, too. It'll give him some respect."

"What good does respect do against McGovern and his crew?"

"That will come next," Clint said. "When you hire a sheriff, he operates better when people have confidence in him. You're going to have to take the lead and show them how to do that."

"And what will you do?"

"I won't wear a badge," Clint said, "but I'll be around."

"You'll help him if he gets in trouble?"

"Yes," Clint said, "if he asks me for help."

"Does he know you're here?"

"Yes, we've already spoken."

"And he didn't ask you for help?"

"Not yet."

"Why not?"

"His pride," Gretchen said.

"Yes," Clint said. He looked at Gretchen. "Do you know him well?"

"Yes," she said, "very well."

"Could I buy you lunch?"

"Why?"

"I'd like to talk about him."

"Why?"

"Because if I'm going to help him," Clint said, "I want to know him."

She studied him for a moment, then said, "All right."

"She can't," Louisa said urgently.

"Why not?"

"She can't go out."

Clint looked at Gretchen.

"Don't listen to her—" she started to say, but the older woman grabbed ahold of Clint's sleeve.

"One of McGovern's men . . . wants her," Louisa said. "She can't go out of the hotel."

"Mother," Gretchen said, "I'll be with Mr. Adams. I'll be all right."

"Yes, yes," Mayor Barnaby said, "don't worry, dear, Mr. Adams will protect her."

Clint could tell from the look in the mayor's eyes that he would have liked nothing more than for Clint to kill one of McGovern's men while protecting his daughter. It would certainly spark a confrontation between Clint and the gang leader.

"You know," Clint said, "all you people had to do was resist, right from the beginning. Just picked up a rifle and fired a few shots, and they would have turned tail and run."

"They would have burned us to the ground!" the mayor said.

"Six men," Clint said, although he wasn't sure of the number, "six men holding an entire town hostage. It's a disgrace."

And it was largely the reason Clint had given up wearing a badge years ago.

SIXTEEN

"There's a café just across the street," Gretchen said to Clint as they left the hotel.

"Are you sure you wouldn't be more comfortable in the hotel dining room?" he asked.

"I have to get out of this hotel," she said. "It's been like a prison. Besides, the food is awful."

"All right, then," he said. "The café it is."

As they crossed the street he said, "Tell me about the McGovern man who's . . . interested in you."

"He's not even a man," she said. "I mean, he is, but he has the mind of a boy."

"Who is it?"

"Virgil McGovern, Frank's brother," she said. "He has a schoolboy crush on me."

"What's wrong with him?"

"There has to be something wrong with him for him to have a crush on me?" she asked.

"I didn't mean—"

She laughed and said, "I know you didn't. I'm sorry, I just . . . I haven't laughed much lately. I don't know what's wrong with Virgil, he's just . . . not right. He's like a little boy."

"What do you do in town, Gretchen—I mean, besides being the mayor's daughter."

"I'm the schoolteacher—although people have pretty much stopped sending their kids to school since the McGoverns arrived."

"Then you're used to dealing with little boys."

"Oh, I can handle Virgil McGovern," she said. "It's the rest of the gang—especially his brother—that bother me."

"They don't scare you?"

They reached the café and stepped inside.

"They don't, except for Frank."

"Why?"

"Let's sit down."

Business was slow—another by-product of the gang's presence in town—and they had their pick of tables. Clint chose one in the back. Gretchen told him the food was very good, so he allowed her to order for both of them.

"Tell me about Frank."

"I thought you wanted to know about Adam?"

"Frank first, then Adam."

"At first sight Frank McGovern is just a bully, a thief, probably a murderer," she said.

"And that scares you?"

"No, that part I understand. It's his relationship with his brother than makes him scary to me."

"Why?"

"He loves him."

"And that scares you?"

"This man is . . . is amoral," she said. "He shouldn't be capable of love. I don't understand it, and so it scares me."

The waiter came with a pot of coffee, filled their cups, and left.

"All right," Clint said, "tell me about Adam Heath."

"What do you want to know?"

"How long have you been in love with him?"

She blushed. "Is it that obvious?"

"Yes."

"Well . . . he came to town about a year ago. I guess I loved him as soon as I saw him."

"And he you?"

"Oh, no," she said. "In fact, we didn't even speak the first few months."

"So when did you become serious?"

"It was gradual," she said, "very gradual. I . . . chased him." She blushed again.

"Why?"

"Because he's wonderful," she said. "He's kind, he's intelligent . . . he came here from New Orleans. Why would he do that? I'd give anything to leave here and go to live in New Orleans."

"Are the two of you talking about marriage?"

"Not seriously . . . not yet."

"Why not?"

"Because he took this damned sheriff's job, that's why!" she said angrily. "He says he can't think of anything else until this job is over."

"And what do *you* say to that?"

"That this job will be over when he's dead." Her eyes started to tear up.

He reached across the table to touch her hand and said, "Not if I can help it."

The food came then. He sat back and gave the waiter room to put it down. It was beef stew, and as Gretchen had promised, it was pretty good.

"Why are you here?" she asked, abruptly. "Why do you want to help us?"

"I didn't come here to help the town."

"Why then? To help Adam?"

He hesitated, then said, "Yes."

"But why? You don't even know him, or you wouldn't be asking me about him."

Clint chewed what was in his mouth slowly, and swallowed. By the time he did he had come to a decision.

"You can't tell anyone what I'm about to tell you, Gretchen."

"All right."

"Not even Adam," he said. "If you tell him he won't thank you for it."

"All right," she said again. "I promise."

"I'm confiding in you—"

"Mr. Adams, I swear what you tell me will go no further," she said testily. "Tell me, already!"

SEVENTEEN

"His mother sent me."

Her eyes widened.

"He never talks about his family. If you know his mother, how is it you don't know him?"

"I knew his mother a long time ago," he said. "Before he was born."

"And she came to you for help?"

"Yes."

"But why?"

"He wrote her, told her he was taking this job."

"He *wrote* to her?" She was incredulous. "He never told me that."

"Gretchen, Adam is at odds with his father."

"I gathered that."

"His father is a wealthy man."

"That doesn't surprise me, either," she said. "I had the feeling he came from money."

"His father has disowned him until he comes back to New Orleans and joins the family business."

"He'd never do that," she said. "He wants to make it on his own."

"That's right," Clint said. "That's why I can't offer him my help; he has to ask for it."

"Oh . . . I don't think he will."

"If he's a smart young man he will," Clint said, "and he'll know when to do it."

"And you'll wait here for that?"

He nodded.

"I promised his mother I wouldn't let any harm come to him, and I intend to keep that promise."

She leaned forward, her tone dropping to a conspiratorial whisper.

"Did you love her? His mother? All those years ago? Is that why she came to you?"

"She came to me," Clint said, "because she knew I could keep him safe."

Gretchen sat back and smiled.

"I'll bet she came to you because she knew you *would* keep him safe, because of the love you shared all those years ago."

"You're a romantic, Gretchen," Clint said. "We shared something years ago, but it wasn't love."

"What was it?"

"Finish your lunch."

"Lust?" she asked, color rising into her cheeks. "Was it lust?"

"Young lady, I'm through answering questions about my past," he said. "Eat your lunch."

"Can we go for a walk after lunch?" she asked.

He frowned at her.

"Oh, I know what you're thinking," she said. "It's what my father was thinking. He's hoping you'll have to kill one of McGovern's men defending my honor."

"And that's not what you want?"

"No, not at all," she said. "I just want to go for a walk. I've been cooped up in that hotel for days. They won't let me leave."

"And where would you like to walk to?"

"Oh, I don't know," she said. "The sheriff's office, maybe?"

"How long has it been since you've seen Adam?" he asked.

"Days!"

"All right." Clint said. "This might be a good idea. We'll go and see him."

"Both of us?"

"Yes."

"He'll want to know why I'm with you."

Clint smiled. "We'll come up with a reason."

EIGHTEEN

Clint could see that Gretchen was both nervous and excited about seeing the young sheriff.

"Just relax," he said, "and remember what I said."

"Don't worry," she said. "He won't find out from me that you know his mother."

They entered without knocking. The chair behind the desk was empty.

"Adam?" Gretchen called.

No answer.

"He's not here."

"I'll check the cells."

He did so and returned without finding Adam. He checked the gun rack on the wall behind the desk and saw that a rifle was missing. Every slot had been filled when he'd been there earlier.

"Where could he be?" Gretchen asked anxiously.

"Relax, Gretchen," Clint replied. "He's probably just out doing his job, making his rounds."

"Alone?"

"He must have done it before since he got the job," he said. "They've been leaving him alone for a while, haven't they?"

71

"That's because they don't see him as a danger," she pointed out.

"Right," Clint agreed. "Once he proves he is. though . . ."

"You've got to help him."

"Let's get you back to the hotel," he said, "and then I'll find him."

"I can get back to the hotel myself," she said. "Just find him."

"No. I told your parents I'd take care of you, and I will. Come on. The sooner I take you back, the sooner I can look for him."

"Let's go. then."

"He's out there." Sam Hawkins said to Frank McGovern.

"Are you sure he's Clint Adams?"

"I'm sure he signed the register as Adams," Hawkins said.

"That don't make him the Gunsmith."

They were in the Number Seven Saloon, the one McGovern had chosen for his base. He had taken the largest room on the second floor for himself and had turned the mayor's house over to his men.

"Okay, let's say it is the Gunsmith," McGovern said. "What would he be doin' here?"

"Passin' through," Hawkins said.

"Or the mayor or somebody sent for him."

"Not since we took over the telegraph office," Hawkins said.

"Right," McGovern said. "Okay, so he's passin' through. What do we do? Leave him alone, or try to recruit him?"

"You think the Gunsmith would work for you? He didn't seem like he had much respect for you."

"Maybe I can change his mind."

"Why? We don't need him."

"What we don't need," McGovern pointed out, "is to have him against us."

"So what are you gonna do?"

"I'm just gonna have a talk with him," McGovern said. "That's all, for now."

"Want me to bring him?"

McGovern laughed.

"You think you can?"

"I can get some of the boys—"

"I'll find him myself," McGovern said. "I don't need to lose any men over this."

"Me and some of the boys can handle him."

"I'm sure you can," McGovern said, and then added, "if he turns out not to be the Gunsmith."

NINETEEN

Once Clint returned Gretchen to the hotel, he went in search of Adam Heath. He figured to simply walk around town until he ran into him. Actually, instead of running into him he saw him, going into a saloon across the street. He crossed over and entered right after him.

"Stopping in for a drink, Sheriff?" he heard the bartender ask Heath.

"No," the young lawman said, "just making my rounds. Everything all right in here?"

"Look around," the barkeep said. "Ain't two men in the whole place. A little early for trouble, yet, Sheriff—unless you want to go looking in the Number Seven Saloon." The way the man said it indicated he knew there was trouble there.

"I'll get there, eventually," Heath said. He turned to leave and saw Clint.

"Hello, Mr. Adams."

"Hello, Sheriff," Clint said. "I was looking for a cold beer, but this doesn't look like the place to get it. What's at the Number Seven?"

"Whiskey, beer, girls, and gambling, I imagine," Heath said. "Oh, I see. You heard the bartender's comment."

"Couldn't help it."

"Well, the Number Seven is where Frank McGovern has decided to hold court—if you know what I mean."

"I do," Clint said. Here was one possible weakness in the boy. He was from New Orleans, well educated, and he might be assuming that he was smarter than most people. Clint had found it easier over the years to simply imagine that everyone was smarter than you were. Let them prove otherwise.

"Maybe I'll check that one out," Clint said. "If McGovern likes it, maybe the beer is the reason."

"Maybe."

"You going over there?"

"Eventually, yes," Heath said. "I still have several places to check first."

"Well then, maybe I'll see you there."

"I'd be careful of McGovern if I was you. Sometimes he and his men are spoiling for a fight."

"They pick a fight with you, yet?"

Heath smiled and said, "They don't take me seriously enough to pick a fight. Yet."

"I see."

"Well," the young man said, "see you there."

Clint let Heath leave the saloon first.

"Damn fool," the bartender muttered.

"Who? The sheriff?" Clint asked.

"What kind of sheriff is that?" the bartender said. "I ask you. Still wet behind the ears. I don't know what the mayor was thinking when he appointed him."

"Maybe he'll be a good man with some experience," Clint said.

"He ain't gonna get any experience in this town."

"Why's that?"

" 'Cause he ain't gonna live long enough," the man said. "Frank McGovern will see to that."

"Did I hear you say McGovern hangs his hat at Number Seven?"

"He does, and you did," the bartender said. "We got cold beer here, though."

"That's okay," Clint said. "I think I'll check on Number Seven."

"Suit yourself."

"I usually do," Clint said, and left.

"Jesus," Sam Hawkins said, staring out the batwing doors of the Number Seven Saloon.

"What is it?" McGovern asked.

"It's Adams," Hawkins said. "Looks like you ain't gonna have to go lookin' for him after all."

"Why's that?"

"He's coming this way."

"How far?"

"Be here in a minute."

"Get out."

"What?"

"You heard me," McGovern said. "I want to talk to him alone. Go on, get out . . . fast, before he gets here."

"Frank—"

"Go!"

Hawkins frowned, but he was out and away from the saloon by the time Clint reached the entrance.

Clint saw Hawkins leave the saloon in a hurry. He didn't know what was up the man's sleeve, but since he apparently wasn't going to be around, Clint put him out of his mind for the moment and approached the batwing doors of the Number Seven Saloon.

TWENTY

When Clint walked in he was surprised to find the place almost deserted. The bartender was behind the bar and there was one man seated at a table. Given the fact that Frank McGovern had chosen this as his base of operation, he assumed that the man was Frank.

"Beer," he said to the bartender.

The barman had already been well trained: He looked at McGovern for permission to give Clint what he asked for.

"Give the man a beer, bartender," McGovern said. "He looks thirsty."

Clint accepted the mug of beer, then turned with it in hand to look at Frank McGovern. He was in his thirties, beefy but not fat. His clothes were clean, probably had come from the general store without paying for them. His gun was more worn, strapped to his right hip.

"You the owner?" Clint asked.

"No, but I run things."

"By whose authority?" Clint asked.

The man laughed.

"You make your own authority, my friend. You ought to know that."

"I should?"

"You're Clint Adams, ain't you?"

"That's right," Clint said. "Do I know you?"

"McGovern," the man said, "Frank McGovern."

Clint snapped his fingers.

"Seems to me I did hear something about you," he said. "What was it . . . oh, yeah, the liveryman told me I didn't want to stop here because of you. What do you suppose he meant by that?"

"I can't imagine," McGovern said. "Tell you what. Why don't you bring that beer over here and drink it with me, and I'll pay for it."

"Can't remember the last time I turned down a free drink," Clint said. He walked to the table and sat opposite McGovern.

"Hey, Mac," McGovern called to the bartender, "bring me a beer, will you?"

The bartender obeyed, but as he served it, he said, "My name's not Mac, it's Jerry."

"Oh, that's right," McGovern said. "I'm the one they call Mac, ain't I?"

The bartender rolled his eyes and went back behind the bar.

"And you're the one they call the Gunsmith," McGovern said to Clint.

"Some do."

"You've got yourself a big rep, Adams."

"Oh, no," Clint said, "you're not one them, are you, McGovern?"

"One of who?"

"One of those people where this conversation is going to end with you inviting me outside?"

"Oh, no," McGovern said, holding his hands up in front of him, "the last thing I'd want to do is face you in a fair fight, Adams. I'm not a fast gun."

"I'm glad to hear it."

"I do have an offer for you, though."

"What kind of offer?"

"First, what are you doin' in town?"

"Passing through," Clint said, then raised his mug and added, "and having a free beer."

"That's all?"

"That's all. Why?"

"I'm gonna offer you a job."

"Doing what?"

"Helpin' me."

"Do what?"

"Keep this town in line."

"You mean you're running the whole town?"

"The whole shebang, yessir."

"With how many men?"

"Me and five others."

Clint decided to stroke the man's ego a bit.

"You mean you and six men have this whole town cowed?" he asked.

"That's right," McGovern said, "although I think I could've done it with less."

"What about the law?"

"Wasn't none when we rode in. Well, that ain't true," he amended. "There was law, but he rode out when we rode in."

"And now?"

"They gave the badge to some wet-behind-the-ears kid who so far don't know what to do with it."

"What are you going to do about him?"

"I ain't decided," the outlaw said. "So far he's been no danger to us. Hell, the town ain't even takin' him serious, why should we?"

"Then why do you need me?"

"Well, we ain't gonna stay here forever. We'll leave eventually to do some work."

"And your work is . . . ?"

"Trains, banks, that sort of thing."

"Oh, well, I'm afraid that's not my work at all," Clint said. "Did you hear someplace that I rob banks and trains?"

"Seems I heard somewhere that you was friends with Frank and Jesse."

Clint's eyes narrowed. "Are *you* friends with Frank and Jesse?"

"No, can't say I am."

"Have you even met them?"

"Nope."

"Then I'll thank you not to call them by their first names as if you had."

McGovern held Clint's gaze for a few moments, then said, "Didn't mean nothin' by it."

At that moment a woman came down the stairs from the second floor. She caught Clint's eye immediately because she was so overly sensuous. Sex radiated from her like heat. She was full-bodied and had a wide, sexy mouth that was now stretched into a quizzical smile.

"Didn't mean nothing by what?" she asked.

"Not now, Mandy," McGovern said.

"Aren't you going to introduce me to your new friend?" she asked.

"We're not friends," Clint said, "but my name is Clint Adams."

"I'm Mandy—" she started, but McGovern cut her off.

"I said not now, damn it! Go back upstairs."

She gave McGovern a hurt look, then looked at Clint again.

"He's not always this horrible," she said. "He must be afraid of you."

With that she turned and went back upstairs, both men watching her hips sway until she was gone.

TWENTY-ONE

"Just because I was friends with Jesse, and am still friends with Frank, doesn't mean I ever robbed a train or a bank in my life. And I'll tell you something else, McGovern."

"What's that?"

Clint stood up for this.

"If I ever decided to start robbing trains and banks it wouldn't be with you."

"Then I guess you're turnin' me down?"

"Flat. I don't want to associate with the kind of man who thinks he can take over a whole town on a whim."

McGovern didn't know what a "whim" was, but it didn't sound good.

"I don't *think* I can take over a town, Adams," he said, "I've done it."

"Well," Clint said, "you may not have it for much longer."

"If you ain't joinin' me, Adams, I'd advise you to think about leavin' town."

"When I've had enough of this place," Clint said, "I'll leave. Not before. Oh, and another thing: Keep your men away from me. Some jasper named Sam Hawkins tried to scare me out of town just by saying your name." He smiled. "That ain't going to do it, McGovern."

"You're askin' for trouble if you stay."

"I never ask for trouble, McGovern."

Clint turned and started walking to the door.

"If you're not with me, you're against me, Adams,"
McGovern called. "Remember that."

"McGovern," Clint said over his shoulder, "I'm not
giving you much thought, at all."

He didn't turn to see what effect this statement had on
the man, but he thought he could predict it. Nobody liked
to be told that they have no effect on someone's life—
especially not a man like Frank McGovern.

After Clint Adams left, Frank McGovern stood up and
threw his full beer mug at the bartender, who ducked just
in time. The mug broke some bottles behind the bar.

"Clean up that mess!" McGovern shouted.

"Yes, sir."

"Who does he think he is," he continued, "talkin' to
me like that?"

"I don't know—"

"I ain't talkin' to you!"

"Yessir."

McGovern sat down and fumed. He wanted one of his
men to walk through the doors, but it didn't happen. He
thought about going out there himself, but he'd meant what
he'd said before. He didn't want to face Clint Adams—not
in a fair fight, anyway.

TWENTY-TWO

Clint was already out of the saloon when he remembered that he had wanted to wait there until Heath showed up. That didn't seem a prudent move, however, given the exchange he'd just had with Frank McGovern.

He crossed the street and stepped into a doorway opposite the saloon. He wanted to be able to intercept the sheriff before he went in; he also wanted to see if McGovern came out and, if so, where he went.

After twenty minutes it was clear McGovern was not coming out. After twenty-five minutes Sheriff Adam Heath appeared down the street, walking toward the Number Seven Saloon.

Clint stepped out of the doorway into the street to intercept him.

"Sheriff!"

"Mr. Adams," Heath said. "Can I help you with something?"

"I wondered if I could talk to you for a minute?"

"About what, sir?"

"It's about Frank McGovern."

Sheriff Heath looked over at the saloon, then back at Clint.

"He's in there, isn't he?"

"Yes. I was just in there and had a conversation with him."

"About what?"

"He offered me a job."

Clint saw the sheriff's eyes narrow and wondered if it was his imagination or if there was something familiar about the gesture.

"Did you take it?"

"I didn't," Clint said. "I don't work for men like him."

Clint saw it in the young man's eyes even before he spoke. He knew what Heath was going to ask him.

"Would you work for me?"

"As a deputy, you mean?"

"Yes."

Clint made a show of thinking about it, then shook his head.

"I won't wear a badge," he said, "but if you're looking for someone to watch your back—"

"You'd have to wear a badge," Heath said, cutting him off. "That's the only way it would be official."

"Why does it have to be official?"

"I try to do everything by the book."

"If the Earps had done things by the book," Clint said, "Doc Holliday wouldn't have been with them in Tombstone. I wonder what would have happened then?"

"I'm not Wyatt Earp."

"Well, I'm not Doc Holliday," Clint said, "but I'll be around."

Heath didn't look comfortable with that. He turned his head and looked at the saloon again.

"You don't want to go in there now," Clint said.

"Why not?"

"Well, for one thing nothing's going on in there," Clint said. "There's only McGovern and the bartender."

"My rounds won't be official until I check it out."

"Sheriff—can I call you Adam?"

"Sure, why not?"

"And you can call me Clint."

"Fine."

"I didn't leave McGovern in the best of moods," Clint said. "If you go in there now it might push him over the edge."

"That might not be a bad thing," Adam said. "We could get this over with."

"Are you ready to face a man like McGovern?"

Adam hesitated, then said, "To tell you the truth, sir—"

"Clint."

"—Clint, I'm really not sure."

"Adam, what experience did you have for this job?"

"None."

"Would you like to learn something about being a lawman?"

"Yes, sir."

"Why don't you discontinue your rounds for now and let's go to your office and talk."

"My rounds won't be official—"

"Official," Clint said, cutting him off. "That's another thing we can talk about."

McGovern was looking out over the batwing doors when Clint Adams caught up with Sheriff Heath. Since Adams had turned him down, what would happen if the sheriff made the offer of a job? That would mean that the sheriff's gun would be backed up by the Gunsmith's.

He watched the two men talk, saw the young lawman look over at the saloon a few times. Finally, though, it seemed that Clint Adams got the young man to turn away and walk off with him.

Initially, McGovern had seen the young man as no threat. Now he realized he might have made a mistake in letting the sheriff live long enough to form an alliance with the Gunsmith.

Frank McGovern decided he might need some more men.

TWENTY-THREE

When Sam Hawkins walked back into the saloon, Frank McGovern started yelling.

"About damn time you got back here!"

"You didn't tell me when you wanted me back—"

"I didn't tell you to get lost, either," McGovern snapped.

"I didn't get lost," Hawkins said. "In fact, I found Virgil wandering around."

"Virgil? Where is he?"

"Outside—hey, Virg? Frank wants you in here."

Virgil appeared at the batwing doors, but he did not enter.

"I ain't comin' in if he's gonna yell," he said.

"He ain't yellin' at you, Virg, he's yellin' at me," Hawkins said.

"I don't want *no* yellin'," Virgil said. "It reminds me of Pa."

"Come on in, Virg," McGovern called, calming himself. "I ain't gonna yell anymore."

"You promise?"

"I promise."

The doors opened and Virgil stepped in. Both he and Frank remembered well how their father used to bellow around the house all the time, usually at their mother, but sometimes at them. And when he was drunk, the old man would start hitting their mother, and the boys would try to stop him. Finally, one day, they stopped him for good. . . .

But that wasn't something Frank wanted Virgil to remember.

"Want a sarsaparilla, Virg?" McGovern suggested.

"Wow! Sure do."

"Mac, or Jay, whatever your name is," McGovern said to the bartender. "Get him one."

Virgil happily went to the bar while McGovern gestured at Sam Hawkins to come closer.

"What happened with Adams?" Hawkins asked.

"We didn't get along," McGovern said. "Look, there's a possibility that Adams might take sides with the new sheriff."

"Why would he put himself out for that punk kid?" Hawkins wondered.

"I don't know," McGovern replied, "but they were talkin' just as sweet as you please out on the street and then they walked away together."

"So what do we do? Warn the other men?"

"Not only that," McGovern said. "I want you to get on the telegraph."

"For what?"

"We need more men."

"Are we payin'?"

"Yeah, we're payin'," McGovern said. "You know who to contact."

"Should I tell them about Adams?" Hawkins asked.

"Hell, no," McGovern said, "let them find out about him when they get here. We don't want to scare 'em away before we can make an offer."

"Okay," Hawkins said, "but you better keep an eye on Virgil."

"Why's that?"

"He was headin' for the hotel."

"The mayor's daughter again?"

Hawkins nodded.

"Can't say I blame him," McGovern said. "She's a pretty little thing."

"That may be," Hawkins said, "but Clint Adams is registered at the same hotel."

"I don't want Adams anywhere near my brother," McGovern snapped.

"That's what I figured," Hawkins said. "Adams might see Virg as a way of gettin' to you."

"Sometimes you're smarter than I give you credit for, Sam," McGovern said. "This is one of those times."

Hawkins wasn't sure if that was a compliment or not.

"Before you go to the telegraph office," McGovern went on, "tell the others to get over here."

"Right."

Hawkins headed for the door.

"Where you goin', Sam?" Virgil McGovern called out. "You said you was gonna take me—"

"I gotta do somethin', Virg," Hawkins said. "Stay here with Frank."

As he went out the door Virgil came over to his brother's table.

"Where's Sam goin', Frank?" he asked. "He was gonna take me to the hotel ta see Miss Gretchen."

"Virgil," McGovern said, "sit down here a minute."

"I gotta go," Virgil said. "Gretchen's waitin'."

"She's not waitin', Virgil," McGovern said. "She doesn't even know that you're alive."

"That ain't true," Virgil said smugly. "She says hello to me. She don't say hello to you."

McGovern thought he'd like to say hello to her, all right, but as long as Virgil was sweet on the mayor's daughter he wasn't about to make a move on her. Besides, he had Mandy to take care of those needs for a while longer. He wasn't *quite* tired of her, yet.

"Virgil," McGovern said, as calmly as he could, "we've talked about this before. . . ."

TWENTY-FOUR

"First of all, have you got a girl?" Clint asked Adam.

"What?"

"A girlfriend," Clint said. "Have you got a girlfriend?"

"Well . . . yes, but what has that got to do—" Sheriff Heath squirmed in his chair. Clint sat across the desk from him.

"You're a serious young man, Adam, aren't you?"

"I suppose so," he replied. "You have to be serious in this job."

"There's such a thing as being too serious," Clint said. "If you have a girl, spend some time with her. Don't ignore her."

"It's too dangerous for her to be seen with me," Adam said.

"See her indoors," Clint suggested. "At her home, at a hotel, whatever."

"A hotel? That would scandalize her and her family," Adam said.

"All right, let's put that aside for now. Let's talk about something else."

"Like what?"

"Like your attitude toward the law."

"What's wrong with my attitude?"

"Nothing," Clint said. "It's perfect—well, yes, all right, *that's* what's wrong with it."

"What?" Adam asked, confused.

Clint leaned forward.

"You don't have to follow every letter of the law," he said. "There are times when you have to bend the rules."

"Like when?"

"Like when you accept help from someone without insisting they become deputized."

"Why do you want to help me?" Adam Heath asked. "You don't even know me."

"You remind me of me," Clint replied. He had anticipated this question and had his answer ready.

"In what way?"

"I've stood against the odds many times, Adam," Clint said. "That's what you're doing now."

"But you always come out on top."

"But there have been times when the odds were stacked too high against me."

"And what did you do then?"

"I accepted help."

"If I accept your help," Adam asked, "what do we do next?"

"Well," Clint said, "accepting my help could also make your problem worse."

"Now you tell me," Adam said. "How?"

"It will probably cause McGovern to take you more seriously."

"If that happens, then it's worth it."

"Because of that," Clint went on, "he might bring in more men."

"You mean . . . the odds could get even worse?"

"It's possible."

"I think I should just take McGovern," Adam said. "He's probably still at the saloon."

"If you take him into custody what do you think the others will do? Leave?"

"I'd hope—"

"Or try to break him out?"

Adam frowned.

"If you want to take him," Clint said, "you'll have to go all the way."

"You mean . . . kill him?"

"When you took this job, didn't you think you might have to kill someone, sometime?"

"I was hoping not."

"I see. You want to be a new breed of lawman, the kind who doesn't kill?"

"Is that so bad?"

"Adam," Clint said, softly, "the time for that kind of a lawman will probably come, but I don't think it's now, and I don't think it's here in Caldwell."

"I can't just walk in and kill him," Adam said. "That'd be murder."

"I'm not suggesting murder."

"What then? Push him into a fight?"

"That probably wouldn't work," Clint said, "not after my conversation with him today. You probably won't find him alone anymore."

"Well, I'm not going to ambush him."

"I'm not suggesting that."

"Then what?"

Clint hesitated, then said, "We'll have to come up with a plan."

"You mean you'll come up a plan and I'll go along?" Sheriff Heath asked.

"Adam," Clint said, "you're the sheriff. The problem here is yours."

"And it's mine because I made it mine," Adam said. "These people needed someone to help them, and I took the job."

"And now you need someone to help you."

"Maybe," Adam said. "Maybe."

"Does that mean you don't want my help?"

"It means that I'll have to give this some thought before I accept your offer."

"All right," Clint said, standing up, "but I think you're forgetting one little thing."

"What's that?"

"I didn't offer my help," Clint said. "You asked me for it."

TWENTY-FIVE

With the first blow, Mandy decided that she'd had enough.
No man was worth this kind of treatment.

She had gone to her room when McGovern insisted, and
he came up soon after. The first thing he did when he entered the room was backhand her across the face.

"Not my face!" she screamed. She touched herself, her
cheek, her nose, then her mouth, checking for blood. Finding none, she dropped her hands and glared at him.

"You're lucky I don't beat you to a pulp," he growled
at her. "Do you know who that man was?"

"No," she said, "but he's obviously someone you're—"

"Don't say it!" he snapped, raising a fist this time.

She cringed and raised her hands, and he lowered his.

"That was Clint Adams," he said, and when she didn't
respond he added, "The Gunsmith, you silly bitch."

"Gunsmith," she said. "I've heard of him."

"Of course you have," he said. "Everybody has."

"What's he doing here?"

"That's what I was trying to find out when you came
barging in."

"And do you know, now?"

"Not exactly."

"Maybe you can get him to work for you."

97

He scowled.

"I tried that already."

"He turned you down?"

"Yes."

He sat on the bed. She could sense he was relaxing. She got on the bed behind him, on her knees, and began to rub his shoulders. He liked that, and she knew what it would eventually lead to.

"Then if he's not with you . . ."

". . . he against me," he finished. "At least you've learned that."

"I've learned a lot more than that," she said, sliding her hands up and down his chest, and then unbuttoning his shirt and slipping her hands inside.

"Lie back," she said in his ear. "I'll relax you."

He sighed, and settled onto his back. She removed his boots, and then his trousers and underwear. He was already half-erect when she touched him, and he sprang to life. She'd seen prettier penises in her time, but never one as large. She had to admit she was fascinated by its size, but even that wasn't worth being slapped around.

She stroked it between her hands until he was fully erect, then stood and dropped her dress to the ground, revealing her opulent flesh to him. She knelt and took his penis between her pillowy breasts and rolled it there, occasionally flicking at it with her tongue. Finally, she settled onto it with her mouth, held it in both hands, and began to suck. She knew she could get him to explode fairly soon, and after that, if he was true to form, he'd fall asleep.

And then she'd go visiting. . . .

TWENTY-SIX

When Clint got back to the hotel he was surprised to find Gretchen waiting for him in the lobby.

"Do your parents know you came back?" he asked.

"Yes, I told them I was back," she said, "and then I came down here to wait for you. What happened? Did you find him?"

Clint looked around and saw a sofa against one wall.

"Let's sit over here."

He took her hand and led her to the sofa.

"Is this going to be bad?"

"Maybe not," Clint said, "but he is a little, uh, stubborn."

"He wouldn't accept your help?"

"Well, actually, he asked for it."

Her face lit up.

"But that's wonderful!"

"But now he doesn't know if he wants it."

Her face fell.

"That's not wonderful. What will you do?"

"I've got to wait for him to make up his mind."

"Maybe if you told him about his mother—"

"No, and you mustn't, either," he said. "Remember your promise."

"I remember," she said. "Don't worry, I'd never tell him unless you agreed."

"We're just going to have to wait a little while."

"How long?"

"Not too long," Clint said, and then told her about his meeting with McGovern.

"The nerve of the man. He actually tried to hire you? That means he's afraid of you."

"Or he just wanted to be able to keep an eye on me," Clint pointed out.

"What happens now that you turned him down?" Gretchen wanted to know.

"Who knows? Men like McGovern are hard to predict. He might come after me, try to get me out of the way."

"Or go after Adam?"

Clint shrugged.

She put her hand on his arm.

"He's so lucky to have you here."

"I hope he thinks so, Gretchen," he said. "Why don't you go back to your room now?"

"I still want to see Adam."

"I'll try to bring him here later," Clint said.

"Promise?"

"Yes, I do."

"All right, then I'll go back upstairs."

They both stood up.

"I wish I knew what this was really about," she said to him.

"What do you mean?"

"I just have a feeling you're not telling me everything, Mr. Adams."

"Clint," he said, "call me Clint, or I won't tell you any more."

"All right," she said, "Clint. Would you like me to tell my father anything?"

"Yes," he said. "Just tell him to stay out of the way."

"There won't be a problem there," she said. "Like most

of the men in Caldwell, he avoids Frank McGovern and his men like the plague.''

''You may see that as a weakness, Gretchen,'' Clint said, ''but if they're not going to fight, the best thing is to lay low.''

''And let somebody else do their fighting for them,'' she added, ''like you.''

''And Adam.''

''Yes,'' she said, ''and Adam.''

She impulsively kissed Clint on the cheek and went up the stairs to her room.

When Clint turned from watching her go, he saw the woman from the saloon, Mandy, standing in the doorway of the hotel.

''Girlfriend?'' she asked.

''No,'' Clint said, ''just a friend.''

''Remember me?''

''Mandy,'' he said, and then added, ''How could I forget?''

She came closer, and she was even more impressive. Her skin was amazingly pale and smooth, and she managed to look as if she were going to bust out of her high-necked dress without looking overweight. She was just . . . ripe.

''I am flattered.''

''What are you doing here?''

''We didn't have a chance to talk when we met.''

''You are Frank McGovern's girl, aren't you?'' he asked her pointedly.

''I am, for now.''

''Then why do you want to talk to me?''

''A girl's got to look out for her future,'' she said, ''and I'm not sure I have one with Frank.''

''What can I do about that?''

''I don't know,'' she said. ''I won't know until we've talked.''

''Do you think it would be wise for us to talk where McGovern can't see us?''

"Oh, yes," she said. "How about your room?"

"How about I buy you a cup of coffee in the dining room, instead?"

She pouted, but said, "Make it tea, and I'll take it."

TWENTY-SEVEN

"If I stand right at the top of the steps," Mandy said, "I can hear what's being said downstairs."

"Wait a minute," Clint said, holding up his hands. "Why would you tell me this?"

She sipped her tea and returned the cup to the saucer. The teacup looked out of place in her hands. She truly belonged in the parlor of an expensive bawdy house. She would have been the most popular girl there.

"I don't trust Frank."

"In what way?"

"I think he's getting ready to get rid of me," she said.

"And?"

"And I want to be the one to walk away. I don't want to be replaced by a younger, prettier model."

"Well," he said, "there may be younger—" She stopped him by putting up her hand, palm out.

"Spare me," she said. "I know what I am. There's younger, there's prettier, but I doubt there's better. *I* know that, but see, men are funny. When it comes to a woman they're like boys who get tired of their toys, no matter how good they are. A little boy will throw away a perfectly good toy for a new one. Men are the same way. Can you argue that?"

"No," he said, "not me. After what I've seen in my life I'd never argue the baser side of men."

"Then there you have it," she said. "That's why I'm telling you this."

"Okay," he said. He surprised himself by being fully prepared to believe what she told him.

"He's bringing in more men," she said. "He's afraid of you. He says he's not, but he is."

"That's no sin," Clint said. "I've been afraid many times in my life."

"Yes, but you're a real man—you admit it. Frank would never admit it."

"That's probably true," Clint said. Admitting fear to himself had kept him alive many times. It kept him from doing anything foolish. "Who's he bringing in?"

"I don't know," she said. "He's leaving that to Sam Hawkins. Sam went over to the telegraph office to take care of it."

"If he's bringing more men in," Clint said, "it means I have time to do the same thing."

"Wow," she said, eyes shining. "You'd bring in somebody famous, wouldn't you?"

"I'd bring in somebody I could trust with my life," Clint said.

"Who would that be?"

"I don't know yet," he replied. "I have to see who's close enough to get here in time."

"How will you know how much time you have left?"

"I'll check with the telegraph operator."

"He'd be too afraid of Frank McGovern to tell you," she said.

He smiled at her and said, "I'll just have to make him more afraid of me, won't I?"

"Well," she said, "If you can scare Frank, I guess you can scare anyone."

After they'd finished their coffee and tea, Clint suggested that Mandy go back to the saloon.

"You sure you wouldn't want me to come to your room with you for a while?" she asked.

"I'd like that a lot," he said. "In fact, when this is all over I'll race you to the nearest bed, but for now I think you better be getting back."

She sighed and said, "Oh, all right . . . but I'll hold you to what you just said."

Smiling, he said, "I'll count on that, Mandy."

TWENTY-EIGHT

After Mandy left Clint went to the sheriff's office to talk to Adam. He hoped that the boy wasn't so headstrong that he wouldn't be there.

"You look surprised," Adam said as Clint entered and saw the young man sitting behind his desk.

"Um, no, not at all."

"You thought I'd be stubborn—or stupid—enough to go and brace Frank McGovern alone, didn't you?"

"Well," Clint said, seating himself, "the thought had crossed my mind."

"Well," Adam admitted, "it crossed mine, too, but I decided against it."

"Good," Clint said. "I've got something to tell you."

"What? Is it about Gretchen? Is she all right?"

"She's fine. She wants you to come by later."

"Tell her I will," he said. "What did you have to tell me?"

"I've got some information that McGovern is sending for more men."

"He's afraid of you."

"He's cautious," Clint corrected him, "maybe even smart."

"So what do we do? Wait for his reinforcements to come?"

"No, we get some reinforcements of our own."

Adam scowled.

"Now what's wrong?"

"I don't know about this," Adam said. "This could cause a shooting war on the streets of Caldwell."

"Adam, what did you think this would escalate into?" Clint asked.

"I . . . I don't know. I guess I . . . I went into this thing with my eyes less than wide open."

"You were hoping that the sight of a man with a badge would change things. That's admirable, Adam, and it may even happen someday."

"But not today."

"No."

"Okay, then," the young lawman said, squaring his shoulders, "what do we do?"

"First I've got to get over to the telegraph office and see if I can find out who Sam Hawkins sent for. What do you know about the men McGovern already has?"

Adam fidgeted in his chair and said, "Not much."

"That's all right," Clint said. "I'll find that out, too."

"You're doing everything," Adam complained.

"Don't worry. You're going to do your share."

"Starting when?"

"Starting now," Clint said. "While I go to the telegraph office, you go and talk to your girl. Tell her you're all right, tell her you love her."

"All right."

"And meet me back here in half an hour."

"Gee, thanks."

TWENTY-NINE

They left the office together, checked the street, and then went their separate ways.

When Clint reached the telegraph office he peered in the window first—he didn't want to run into Sam Hawkins. When he saw it was empty he went inside. The clerk reacted with a start, then relaxed when he saw that it wasn't one of McGovern's men.

"Can I help you, sir?"

"Yes," Clint said. "Was Sam Hawkins in here today?"

"Hawkins?"

"McGovern's man."

Now the fear crept back into the man's eyes.

"Are you—"

"One of McGovern's men?" Clint finished. "No, I'm not, but I do need to see the telegram Hawkins just sent."

"Why?"

"Look," Clint said, "I don't have time to explain. My name is Clint Adams."

The man's eyes widened.

"The Gunsmith?"

"That's right."

"Why are you here?"

"To help this town get out from under the McGovern Gang."

"It's about time somebody came who—"

"I'm working with your new sheriff."

"Adam Heath?"

"That's right."

"You ain't takin' over?"

"No, I'm just here to help him—and you."

"Well," the man said, frowning, trying to understand why the Gunsmith wouldn't take over from a young, inexperienced lawman, "I guess that's better than nothing. All right, what can I tell you?"

"Did Hawkins send a telegram?"

"He sent four."

"To who?"

"Hold on."

The clerk went to another part of the desk and came back with four flimsy sheets of paper.

"Here they are."

Clint took them and scanned each until he found what he wanted: the names.

"All right," he said, handing them back, "take a telegram from me."

"Yes, sir."

"To Rick Hartman, Labyrinth, Texas. Need information on the following names: Randall Trapp, Terry Tremayne, Claude Snipes, and Ed Sherman. As soon as possible. That's it," he told the man. "You put in the stops. I never know where they're supposed to go."

"I'll take care of it, sir."

"And if anyone comes in and asks if I sent a telegram . . ."

"You can count on me not to say a word, sir."

"Sure," Clint said, thinking, *Until somebody scares you enough to talk.*

"Any more, sir?"

"Not yet," Clint said. "I need that reply as soon as it

comes in. Bring it to the hotel, or to the sherriff's office."

"Yes, sir."

"On second thought, take it to the sheriff's office and give it to the sheriff."

"Yes, sir."

"And treat him with the same respect you're treating me with. He's going to save this town."

"Adam Heath?" the man said, incredulously.

"That's right," Clint said. "Sheriff Adam Heath."

With that he walked out.

THIRTY

"Did you get those telegraph messages sent?" Frank Mc-
Govern asked, as he came down the stairs from the second
floor of the saloon. He had awakened, found Mandy gone,
and gotten dressed.

"I did it," Hawkins said, from his table.

Around the room sat the other men. Larry Doby was
sitting with Hawkins while the other two men, Tom Kennedy and Trent Mead, were sitting together.

Virgil was sitting between Hawkins and Doby, but for
the moment he seemed oblivious to what was going on
around him. It was only the sound of his brother's voice
that snapped him out of it.

"Hi, Frank!"

"Hi, Virgil," McGovern said, moving to the bar. The
bartender automatically put a beer on the bar for him. Mc-
Govern took it, then joined his brother at the table with
Doby and Hawkins.

"Who did you get?"

"I sent word to four men," Hawkins said. "We still got
to hear back from them."

"Who are they?"

"Randall Trapp, Terry Tremayne, Ed Sherman, and
Claude Snipes."

"Never heard of any of them," Kennedy piped up.

"They're all good men," McGovern said.

"And they're all within a day or two's ride," Hawkins put in.

"What's goin' on, Frank?" Mead asked. "How much longer are we gonna hang on here?"

"Not much longer," McGovern said.

"Then why are you sending for more men?" Kennedy asked.

"Two words," Hawkins said. "Clint Adams."

That made Kennedy and Mead sit up straight.

"The Gunsmith?" Kennedy said.

"He's here?" Mead asked.

"That's right," McGovern said, "and he's siding with the new sheriff."

Kennedy and Mead exchanged a panicky look.

"We got to get out," Kennedy finally said.

"We got to leave," Mead said.

"I'll kill the first man who moves," McGovern said. "What the hell's the matter with you two?"

"This is the Gunsmith we're talkin' about," Kennedy said.

"Livin' in the mayor's house ain't worth facing him," Mead added.

"It ain't huh?" McGovern asked. "What if I threw in the mayor's daughter?"

That stopped Mead. He'd had eyes for Gretchen ever since they got to town, but McGovern had warned him off because he knew his brother had a crush on her.

"Gretchen?" Virgil said.

"Quiet, Virgil," McGovern said.

"But Frank—"

"Shut *up*, Virgil!"

Virgil fell into a sullen silence.

"We're getting reinforcements, and the Gunsmith is only one man," McGovern said.

"What about the sheriff?" Kennedy asked.

"He's a kid."

"He's got a gun." Kennedy said.

"We'll give Virgil a gun." McGovern said. "That should square things."

"How many will we be?"

"Ten. at the most." Hawkins said.

"We'll be ten." McGovern said. "The others will show." He looked at Kennedy and Mead. "What do you say?"

They exchanged a glance. then Mead said. "We'll stay. Frank."

"There's my boys." McGovern said.

In the silence that followed. Virgil suddenly asked. "I get a gun?"

THIRTY-ONE

Clint was waiting in the office when Adam returned from seeing Gretchen.

"How did it go?"

"She cried," Adam said.

That didn't sound like the Gretchen Clint had come to know in such a short time—but then, he'd never seen the two of them together.

"She still wants me to give up the badge."

"And what did you say?"

"I said no, especially not now that I have you here to help me."

"That must have made me one of her favorite people," Clint said, as Adam seated himself at his desk.

"What did you find out?" the sheriff asked.

"Four names," Clint replied. "Trapp, Tremayne, Sherman, and Snipes."

"Claude Snipes?"

"That's right," Clint said. "You know him?"

"I think I saw a poster on him," Adam said. "There's not much else to do here but read posters." He opened a drawer, took out a pack of wanted posters, and started going through them. "Here he is." He handed one across the desk to Clint.

"Claude Snipes," Clint read, "bank robbery, train robbery . . . one, two . . . three states."

"Kansas?"

"No."

"Here's another one," Adam said. "Randall Trapp." He handed it across.

"Bank robbery . . . murder."

"Murder? If he comes here I can arrest him."

"You're not looking to make any extra arrests, Adam," Clint said. "You want these men to clear out. I mean, you'd prefer that to killing them, wouldn't you?"

"I suppose."

"Do have any intention of making this a career?" Clint asked. "I mean, law enforcement?"

"Well, no."

"So then you're not looking to make a name for yourself from this."

"That was never my intention," Adam said. "I just wanted to help the town."

"And maybe impress Gretchen and her father, so he'd approve of you?"

Adam fidgeted in his chair and said, "Maybe."

"Any more posters?"

Adam looked down at them as if seeing them for the first time, then gathered them up and said, "Oh, no, just those."

"Well," Clint said, looking at the posters on Trapp and Snipes, "at least we have some idea of what we'll be dealing with."

He handed them back. Adam added them to the others and put them all back in his drawer.

"It'll take these men a few days to get here," Adam said. "And the same goes for anyone you contact, right?"

"Right," Clint said, "and I think I know where you're going with this."

"If we forced the issue we could handle it now, with a minimum of shooting."

"Well, what that means is that we'd have less men with guns shooting up the town."

"Right."

Clint rubbed his jaw. "We could do it that way," he said. "Then the question becomes, is McGovern pushable? Or will he prefer to wait? Like you said, you don't want to just walk up to him and start shooting."

"But if we both approached him we could probably take him."

"What do you mean by 'take him'?" Clint asked.

"I mean put him in a cell," Adam said. "I don't mean kill him."

"What do you think the others would do then?" Clint persisted. "We talked about this before, Adam. They're not just going to stand around and let you take him. If you start something, you're going to have to be willing to go all the way."

"I . . . don't know about that."

Clint stood to leave and said, "Let me know when you do."

THIRTY-TWO

"Where have you been?" Frank McGovern demanded when Mandy entered the saloon.

The other men stared at her except for Virgil. He thought she was a "painted lady," and he didn't like them. He thought they were "evil."

"I went shopping."

"You didn't buy anything."

"I didn't see anything I wanted."

He grabbed her arm as she went by the table.

"You always see something to buy."

She pulled her arm away and said, "I think I've bought everything that's worth buying in this town. I'm going upstairs."

He watched her go to the steps and then turned and found the others watching her, too. They all quickly looked away. He looked at Hawkins, who simply shook his head.

"I'm gonna have to get rid of that woman," McGovern said.

"Pass her over to me," Doby said, but he turned away when McGovern glared at him.

"Okay," McGovern said, "get out—and stay out of trouble. Don't even think about picking on that kid sheriff. I don't want any trouble until the others get here."

"We always stay out of trouble," Kennedy protested.

"Yeah," McGovern said, "right. What about that sheriff and deputy in Tucson?"

"I shot the sheriff," Kennedy said, "but I didn't shoot the deputy."

THIRTY-THREE

Clint was still at the sheriff's office, drinking coffee with Adam, when the telegraph operator arrived with the reply from Rick Hartman.

"I don't know how you can drink this stuff," Adam was saying, frowning at the coffee. "It's too strong. I prefer tea."

Maybe this wasn't his son, after all, Clint thought.

The operator said, "I have that answer for you, Mr. Adams."

"Answer to what?" Adam asked.

"Thanks," Clint said, and gave the man a tip.

"Thank you, sir."

"Remember what we talked about."

"My lips are sealed."

"What answer?" Adam asked again, as the man left.

"I asked a friend of mine to get some information on the four men."

"What's he say?"

Clint scanned the reply and said, "Pretty much what the posters said. The other two are of the same type." He folded it and put it in his pocket. "He says to be careful."

"Does he think you need to be told that?"

"Sometimes he does, yes."

Adam put down his half-finished mug of coffee with every intention of never picking it up again.

"So?"

"So what?"

"Are you going to send for help?"

Clint put his chin in his hand.

"Or are we going to force the issue? It's your call. You have the experience," Adam pointed out.

Clint was surprised at how quickly the young man had put the matter into his hands. He got up and walked to the window, looking out just as Sam Hawkins and another man walked past across the street.

"Do you know all of McGovern's men on sight?" he asked Adam.

"Yes, why?"

Clint turned and faced him, smiling.

"What's that smile about?" Adam asked.

"I'm thinking McGovern has probably told his men to stay out of trouble and to stay out of our way, until the others arrive."

"So?"

"So if we push, they may not push back, but if we push hard enough . . ."

". . . they won't be able to resist."

"He would," Clint said. "McGovern would hold himself in check, and Hawkins might, but maybe not the rest."

"So we push them until they react, and then we arrest them."

"If we can get them all in a cell, we'll only have Hawkins and McGovern to deal with."

"Two against two," Adam said, "but what about when the rest arrive?"

"By the time they do," Clint replied, "there won't be anyone left to pay them—and they're not coming here out of friendship."

Adam thought it over for a few moments and then said, "This is a good plan."

"I think so."

Now Adam grinned.

"So when do we start?"

"Why wait?"

"A great woman once said, 'There's no time like the present.' "

"Really? Who?"

"I can't remember right now."

"That's okay," Clint said. "It's good advice, anyway."

THIRTY-FOUR

Clint and Adam left the sheriff's office in time to see Hawkins split off from not one, but two other men and go his own way.

"Kennedy and Mead," Adam said, identifying them. "They rode in with McGovern."

"Who else is there?" Clint asked.

"Hawkins, Larry Doby, Virgil McGovern, and Frank himself."

Clint nodded and kept his eyes on the two men. Once Hawkins left them they seemed undecided about where to go or what to do.

"You know," Adam began, "it would really get Frank's goat if we arrested Virgil."

Clint looked at Adam.

"That would push him over the edge."

"Does he know about you and Gretchen?" Clint asked unexpectedly.

Adam frowned.

"I don't know. It's no secret in town. He might. Why do you ask?"

"Because if you grab somebody he loves," Clint said, "he'll grab somebody you love."

"God," Adam said. "I can't expose Gretchen to that."

"Then we won't," Clint said. "Come on, they're on the move."

They followed the two men.

"Can I really have a gun, Frank?" Virgil asked his brother when the others had left.

"We'll see, Virg."

"I ain't never had a gun before," Virgil said. "Not a loaded one."

"I know, Virg."

"Frank?"

"Yeah, Virg."

"You ain't gonna yell at me no more, are ya?"

"Not if you listen to me, Virg."

"I'll listen," Virgil said. "I promise."

"That's good, Virg. You know what Momma always said about promises."

"Yes, sir, I do," Virgil said. " 'A promise made is a promise kept.' "

"That's right, Virg."

"I'll keep it, Frank."

"I know you will, Virg," McGovern said, "but now there's somethin' I want you to do for me."

"What's that, Frank?"

"I want you to keep quiet for a while so I can think. Can you do that for me?"

"Sure, Frank," Virgil said. "I can keep quiet."

"Good," McGovern said. "Do it."

"Okay, Fr—" Virgil began, then caught himself and clapped both hands over his mouth.

"That's good, Virg," McGovern said, "that's real good."

In the ensuing silence Frank McGovern started thinking about all of his problems, the worst being Clint Adams, the least being when to get rid of Mandy.

•   •   •

Clint and Adam followed the two McGovern men to a saloon at the far end of town.

"Do you know the place?" Clint asked.

"Real small," Adam said, nodding.

"Back door?"

He thought a moment, then nodded and said, "I think so."

"You *think* so?"

Adam closed his eyes, visualizing the place, then opened them and said, "I'm sure."

"I hope you are," Clint said, "because that's the way I'm going in."

"And me?"

"You," Clint said, "you're going in the front."

THIRTY-FIVE

Clint went around the small saloon and was relieved to find that it did indeed have a back door. However, it was locked, and it took him a few precious moments to force it open. Whether or not young Adam Heath was his son, he had sent the youngster in the front door to face those two men alone.

He finally entered the back of the saloon. Once inside, he could hear voices from the front and followed the sounds down a hall. He found himself looking out a doorway that was just to the left of the bar. McGovern's two men, Kennedy and Mead, were standing at the bar, and Sheriff Adam Heath was standing just inside the batwing doors. Luckily, everyone's eyes were on the lawman.

"Whew!" Adam said. "Jesus, I was wondering what the stench was coming from in here, and now I know."

"Sheriff," the bartender said, "ain't no smell in here."

"Sure there is, bartender," Adam said, "and it's coming from them. They must be McGovern men."

Clint could see that they were both getting red in the face.

"Sheriff," Mead said, "we just come in here to have a drink together, that's all."

131

"Together?" Adam repeated. "Oh, I see. You fellas want to be . . . *together*."

His meaning was clear in the tone of his voice, and the two men grew even redder. Kennedy was the first to speak.

"Now look here, boy—" he started.

"Boy?" Adam cut him off. "Is that the way you address an officer of the law? As boy?"

"That's right," Kennedy said, "when the officer of the law is a little shit—"

"Don't—" Mead said to his partner, but the damage was done.

"You know," Adam said, "talking that way to an officer of the law is against the law. I'm going to have to take both of you in."

"Both of us?" Mead asked. "What the—"

"Just put your guns on the bar, boys, and step away from them."

With those words the bartender suddenly moved all the way to one side of the bar.

"Are you talkin' to us . . . boy?" Kennedy asked. "You're standin' there alone, facing the two of us, your gun not even out, and you're talkin' to us that way?"

"Kennedy, he's tryin' to start somethin'—" Mead warned.

"Well, he succeeded, Mead," Kennedy said, " 'cause I ain't walkin' peacefully to jail . . . are you?"

Mead thought about it a moment, then said, "Well, no, damn it, I ain't."

"You boys are under arrest," Adam said. "Are you coming?"

"No, we ain't," Kennedy said.

"Well then, that's resisting arrest. I'm going to have to add another charge."

"Why don't you just pull out that hogleg, Sheriff," Kennedy taunted, "and we'll settle this right here."

"I'm afraid I can't do that, boys."

"You yella?" Mead sneered.

"No, that isn't it," Adam said. "It's just that my friend had something else in mind."

"What friend?" Mead asked.

"Me," Clint said, and stepped out from the back.

Kennedy and Mead must have been riding together a long time, because Kennedy kept his eyes on Adam while Mead turned around to see who was behind them.

"Shit," he said.

"What?" Kennedy asked.

"The Gunsmith," Mead said.

"How do you know?"

"I seen him once."

"You sure?"

"Yep," Mead said, "it's him."

"I think the sheriff said something about putting your guns on the bar, boys," Clint said. "What do you say?"

"We'll do it," Mead said, "but McGovern ain't gonna like this."

"We'll worry about McGovern," Adam said. "Just set your guns on the bar and step away from them."

"Sheriff," Kennedy said, "you got no call to arrest us."

He and Mead took out their guns, set them on the bar, and stepped away from them.

"You insulted an officer of the law," Adam said, "and then you resisted arrest."

"Insults ain't no offense," Mead said.

"Why don't we let a judge decide that?" Clint suggested.

"Judge?" Mead asked. "What judge?"

"There should be a circuit judge riding into here, oh, in about two weeks or so," Adam said.

"You're gonna keep us locked up for two weeks?" Kennedy asked incredulously. "For callin' you boy?"

Adam looked at Clint. "Is that about right?"

"Sounds like as good a reason as any to me," Clint replied.

THIRTY-SIX

Adam put the two men in a cell while Clint deposited their guns on the sheriff's desk. He was leaning against the desk when Adam came back, and he beamed at the young man.

"What?"

"I was real proud of you back there," Clint said. "You stood up to them just fine."

"Well . . . I knew you were back there."

"I almost wasn't."

"What?"

"That back door was locked."

Adam took off his hat and ran a hand through his hair.

"Well, I guess I'm glad I didn't know that," he said finally.

"You had no way of knowing if I was really there or not," Clint said, "and you still stood up to them."

"Yeah, well, they only backed down when you stepped out."

"That doesn't matter," Clint said. "You did your job, Adam. You did it just fine."

"Well," the younger man said, reddening a bit from the praise, "thanks. Now that we have these two in a cell, though, what do we do? Let McGovern know?"

"Well, we don't let him know as much as we let him find out," Clint replied, and then explained. . . .

Clint and Adam went to the saloon nearest the Caldwell House Hotel, got a couple of beers, and sat at a back table. They proceeded to have a loud conversation about "those two McGovern men" and "the looks on their faces when we locked them up." They repeated the scene in a couple of other saloons—certain that by the end of the day, the information would get back to McGovern.

"Now what do we do?" Adam asked, when they were finished with their "act" and had gone back to the jail.

"Well, I'm going over to the hotel to get my gear," Clint said.

"Why's that?"

"Because you and I are going to spend the night right here," Clint said. "Just in case. Do you need to pick up anything?"

"Not really," Adam said, "except I'm a little hungry."

"I'll bring something back from the hotel."

"If we're going to be stuck here, I'll need some tea."

"Tea," Clint repeated.

"Yep," Adam said, "tea."

"I'll bring some tea." Clint eyed the gun rack. "Are all those weapons in working order?"

Adam looked at them and said, "I don't know. I haven't had to use them all—"

"Check them out while I'm gone," Clint ordered. "If any of them aren't working, we need to know it."

"Okay."

Clint walked to the door.

"Don't open the door for anyone but me."

"All right."

"Anyone!"

"I said all right."

"Not even if they say it's Gretchen."

"All right, Clint," Adam said, "I get it."

Clint stared at the younger man, shook his head, said, "Tea," again, and went out.

THIRTY-SEVEN

Sam Hawkins went looking for Kennedy and Mead; when he couldn't turn them up, he checked in at the little saloon—where he heard they'd been arrested. He couldn't believe his ears.

"Sure thing, Mr. Hawkins," the bartender told him. "Took 'em slicker 'n spit. One came in the front door, and one the back."

"Who came in the front?"

"The sheriff."

Hawkins slammed his palm down on the bar, turned, and stalked out.

McGovern just stared at Hawkins while the man gave him the news.

"Sons of bitches!" he swore. "You think they know we sent for more men?"

"I guess I could check with the telegraph operator."

"Don't bother," McGovern said. "He might lie, you might have to pay him or hurt him. It ain't worth the effort. Besides, he just brought me these." He held up four telegrams.

"All four?" Hawkins asked.

"They're all coming," McGovern confirmed. "One tomorrow, the other three the day after."

"What do we do in the meantime?" Hawkins asked. "About Kennedy and Mead?"

"I think the sheriff and Adams are trying to push me," McGovern said. "I don't like being pushed."

"So are we gonna break them out?"

"No, stupid," McGovern said, "that's what they're trying to push me into."

"So what do we do?"

"We just sit tight and wait for the others."

"What if Adams and the sheriff come after me or Doby? Or even Virgil?" Hawkins wanted to know.

"You'll all move in here," McGovern said. "But I think Adams and the sheriff will be staying at the jail all night."

"Why?"

"Waiting for us to try to break Kennedy and Mead out."

"But we're not."

"No," McGovern said, "we're not . . . yet."

Mandy was standing at the top of the steps, listening to the conversation between Frank McGovern and Sam Hawkins. She knew that Virgil was down there, also. She'd heard Frank get Virgil to be quiet by dangling the possibility of a gun in front of him. She knew that would never happen. Frank was much too worried that his idiot brother might shoot himself with a loaded gun.

As she listened, she felt she was in possession of information that would help Clint Adams. What she had to do now was get out of the saloon—and then back—without Frank noticing she was gone.

She listened intently for some indication of what he was going to do over the next few hours.

"You and Larry bring your gear here and get settled upstairs," McGovern said.

"What about me, Frank?"

"You're staying here with me, Virg," his brother said.

"We'll play some cards until the boys get back."

"Oh, good," Virgil said, "I like cards."

That suited Mandy fine. If Frank was going to stay with his brother, she had time to slip out and back without him being the wiser.

She went back to her room for a shawl.

THIRTY-EIGHT

When the knock came at the jail door, Clint had just returned with his rifle and saddlebags. He hadn't checked out of the hotel, though, preferring to keep the room for later use.

"Who could that be?" Adam asked. "Gretchen?"

"I hope not," Clint said. "She shouldn't be out walking around." He went to the door. "Who is it?"

"Mandy," an anxious voice answered. "Let me in before someone sees me."

Clint looked at Adam, who was frowning, and then unlocked the door and let her in. As she slipped past him, he instantly reacted to the smell of her. It was amazing, but this woman seemed to be walking sex.

"Clint," Adam said, "that's—"

"I know who she is," Clint said. "What are you doing here, Mandy?"

"I heard something I thought you should know," she said, but then she turned her head and looked at Adam and the cup he was holding. She sniffed the air. "Is that tea?"

"Yes, it is," Adam said. "Would you like a cup?"

"I don't—well, yes, I would. I haven't even seen tea in—well, a very long time."

"I just made this one," he said, holding it out to her. "It has two sugars. Is that—"

"That's perfect," she said. She walked to him and took the cup. "Thank you."

She turned to face Clint.

"So what did you hear?" he asked.

"The other four men Frank sent for have agreed to come to town."

"When?"

"One tomorrow, three the day after."

"How has Frank reacted to us putting two of his men in a cell?"

"He's amazingly calm about it," she replied. "It's Sam Hawkins who's worked up about it. Frank just thinks you're trying to push him into making a mistake."

"Well," Clint said, "he's right about that, but I guess he's not going to push so easy."

"The only way to get to Frank," Mandy said, "is through his idiot brother."

"That's what I said," Adam remarked.

"He'd be hard to get to, though," she continued. "Frank is moving the rest of the men into the saloon. He says he figures you two will hole up here."

Clint looked at Adam.

"He's smart," he said. "I hadn't counted on that."

"I have to get back before he notices I'm gone," she said. She sipped the tea, then handed it back to Adam. "It's delicious. Thank you."

"Be careful," Clint said.

At the door, she turned and impulsively kissed him on the mouth. Her lips were full and supple, and she tasted sweet.

"Remember our agreement," she said, and left.

"What agreement was that?" Adam asked. "How did you get her on our side?"

"I didn't," Clint said. "She came to me."

"And this agreement you made with her?"

"It's nothing," he said.

"Nothing?"

"It's personal," Clint said, "for after this is all over with."

"Oh," Adam said, suddenly understanding, "that kind of personal."

"Yes," Clint said, "that kind. Are you going to make more tea, or drink that one?"

Adam looked at the cup in his hand, then said, "I'll drink this one. She only had one sip."

"Then I'm going to make my coffee."

"The stove is yours," Adam said, and sat behind his desk with his tea.

THIRTY-NINE

Clint took advantage of the situation to try and get Adam to talk about himself.

"What brought you here, Adam?" he asked.

"Boredom, I suppose."

"Bored with New Orleans?"

"Who told you I was from—oh, did Gretchen tell you that?"

"She did."

"Well . . . I guess I let that slip one night," he said. "Girls have a way of getting things out of you."

"Yes, they do," Clint said. "Was that something you wanted to keep from her?"

"I just . . . don't like to talk about myself," Adam said.

"Yourself?" Clint asked. "Or your family?"

Adam stared at nothing for a while, then shrugged and said, "Both, I suppose."

"Why's that?"

"I guess I don't much like where I came from."

"New Orleans?"

"No, I mean the kind of family I came from."

"What's wrong with your family?"

Adam didn't answer, preferring to look down.

"Do you love your mother?" Clint asked.

His head came up quickly.

"I love my mother very much," he said. "She's the best part of me."

"Then that would make your father . . . the worst?" Clint asked.

Adam hesitated, then looked directly into Clint's eyes, his expression serious.

"If I tell you something, will you swear not to tell anyone else?"

"Not if you don't want me to."

"He's not my father."

"Who?"

"The man I grew up thinking of as my father."

Now, Clint found this interesting. How had the young man come to that conclusion?

"Why do you say that?"

"I look at my father," Adam said, "my brothers, my sister—I'm the oldest, and I'm nothing like them, they're nothing like me. I'm nothing like *him*."

"That doesn't mean—"

"There's more."

"Like what?"

"My birthday," he said. "When I compare my birthday to their wedding date, something doesn't figure."

Clint frowned. Could Olivia have been that careless when preparing Adam's birth certificate? And if Adam could figure it out, wouldn't his "father" have figured it out as well?

"So what you're saying is . . ."

". . . I have a different father than they do," he finished. "Troy Heathcote is not my real father."

"Then who is?"

"I wish I knew," Adam said.

"What would you do if you did find out?"

Adam fidgeted in his chair.

"I've thought about that a lot," he said, finally. "First

I thought I'd kill the bastard for leaving us, for letting my mother marry Troy Heathcote.''

"And then?"

"And then I thought I'd give him a chance to explain," Adam said, "and *then* kill him."

"Why don't you ask your mother to explain?"

"That would embarrass her," he replied. "I love my mother; I forgive her already without asking her to explain. I'd never shame her like that. She must have thought she had a good reason to keep it from me."

"And what about his reasons?"

"Those I'd like to hear," Adam said.

"And then you'd kill him?"

"No," the young sheriff said, shaking his head, "I've decided that no matter what happens I can't kill my own father."

"That's good."

"But I don't have to speak to him," he went on, "or have anything to do with him once he's told me his story."

"You mean that whatever his story is, you'll never forgive him?" Clint asked.

"Never," Adam said.

"That's pretty harsh, Adam."

"That may be," he said, "but some time in the last twenty-two years he could have made contact with me, instead of letting me go through life feeling fatherless."

Clint frowned.

"When did you figure all of this out?"

"Years ago," Adam said, "I was in my early teens when I did the math, when I looked around and noticed how very different I was from the rest of the family."

"How do your brothers and sisters feel about you?" Clint asked.

"They love me," he said, "and I love them. We do have the same mother, so we're still brothers and sister, even if it's just by half."

"And what about the man who raised you?"

"He must have known all along, too," he said, "because he never made me feel loved. Oh, he wanted me in the family business, but that was for appearances. See, I knew if I went to work for him I'd never have anything really important to do. To the world outside—to New Orleans society—I would look like the dutiful older son going into the father's business, but I'd never really have anything to do with it."

"So rather than be some sort of figurehead," Clint said, "you decided to move out here."

"I decided to go West," Adam corrected him. "I was heading for California, but I stopped here, and I saw Gretchen." The expression on his face changed completely. "I took one look at her, heard her voice once, and knew I could never leave here without her."

"So you still intend to go to California?" Clint asked.

Adam nodded and said, "With Gretchen as my wife, if she'll have me."

"And did you think that taking this job would impress her?"

"I hoped it would."

"You're a foolish young man, Adam."

"Why's that?"

"Because the girl is already in love with you," Clint said. "Anyone can see that. She'd leave with you tomorrow, if you asked her."

"Do you really think so?"

"Son," Clint said, calling him that for the first time, "I know so."

FORTY

When Mandy entered her room above the saloon she found Frank McGovern there, lying on the bed fully dressed, waiting for her.

"Where've you been?" he asked her.

"I went . . . for a walk."

"Where?"

"Just around." She removed her wrap.

"It's dangerous to walk around town alone," he said. "Since when did you start that?"

"I've done it a few nights."

McGovern scared her by bounding off the bed with the speed of a cat and squeezing her face in one hand.

"Why don't I believe you?"

"I . . . don't . . . know," she said with an effort because he was hurting her.

He grabbed one of her breasts with his other hand and began to cruelly twist it.

"Let's see if we can figure out a way for you to convince me," he said.

With Frank McGovern upstairs waiting for Mandy, and both Hawkins and Doby settling into their rooms, Virgil

151

seized the opportunity to sneak out and go to see his girl-friend, Gretchen.

When he entered the hotel, the doorman saw him and cringed. Virgil liked that. The people in town were afraid of him and Frank. Frank said that was because the people knew that he and Virgil were stronger than they were. Virgil liked the idea of being strong.

He walked down the hall to the door of Gretchen's room, already knowing the room number. He knocked gently on the door because he didn't want to frighten her.

"Who is it?" she called.

"It's me," he said, totally unaware that this would probably get almost anybody to open their door to see who it was. He was simply stating a fact. It *was* him.

He heard the lock click and then the door opened. When she saw him, her eyes widened and she tried to slam the door, but he was too quick. He shouldered it open and entered the room.

"Virgil," she said, "you have to get out of here."

"But I came to see you," he said. "I miss you."

"Virgil—"

"You look so pretty," he said, his gaze moving up and down her body hungrily.

Suddenly, she became aware that she was wearing a nightgown, and folded her arms across her breasts.

"Don't hide from me, Gretchen," he said. "You're my girlfriend."

"I'm not, Virgil."

"Yes, you are," he said, approaching her, "you are." He reached for her, his hands suddenly looking impossibly large.

"Virgil—" she said, but she didn't get any further. He took hold of her arms and pulled them away from her breasts. In doing so, his fingers got hooked in the bodice of the gown and tore it away. Her young, firm breasts bobbed into view, and Virgil's mouth went dry. He'd never seen anything so pretty before.

"Gretchen . . ."

"Virgil, don't!" she cried, trying to cover herself.

This made him angry. He pulled her hands away again and grabbed her breasts. Her flesh felt smooth and hot to him. Not knowing his own strength, he squeezed her too hard, and she screamed.

Frank McGovern didn't hear the scream. That was because Mandy was doing some screaming of her own as he twisted the nipple of one of her breasts.

Hawkins and Doby didn't hear Gretchen's scream because they were both listening to Mandy's.

Clint and Adam heard the screams.

"Who was that?" Adam said, coming up out of his chair.

"Sounded like two different women," Clint said.

"Gretchen!" Adam said, and ran for the door.

"Adam, it may have been Mandy," Clint called. "Don't. One of us has to stay—"

But there was no stopping young Sheriff Adam Heath. He was out the door, gun in hand, on his way to the hotel to save his girl.

Clint felt the whole thing could have been a ruse to get them out of the jail, but then he heard screams again, and then there was a gunshot—just one gunshot, and it couldn't have been Adam's, because he couldn't have reached the hotel yet.

Clint ran out and headed for the Number Seven Saloon.

FORTY-ONE

Adam Heath burst into the lobby of the hotel and shouted at the clerk, "Where did the shots come from?"

"I don't know, I don't know!" the frightened man screamed. "Upstairs."

Adam ran up the stairs and saw that two room doors were open down the hall. When he reached them, he realized one was the room where the mayor and his wife were staying, and the other was Gretchen's.

As he ran past the mayor's room he saw it was empty. He turned and looked into Gretchen's room, and found them. She and her parents were standing over a still form.

"Gretchen?" he said.

She ran into his arms. He looked at her father over her head as he held her close to him and noticed the gun in the man's hand for the first time. "What happened?" he demanded.

"He was attacking her," Mayor Barnaby said. He looked at the gun in his hand, then added, "I shot him."

"Who?" Adam asked, trying to catch a glimpse around the sobbing girl.

"It's—it's Virgil McGovern," Gretchen said, her face against his shirt.

"Oh, Lord," her mother said, "they'll kill us now for sure."

Clint ran into the saloon and looked at the bartender.

"Did the shot come from here?"

"No, sir."

"The screams?"

"Well—"

Clint started for the stairs, but before he got there he saw Frank McGovern coming down.

"What was that shooting?" McGovern asked.

"I don't know," Clint said. "I thought it came from here."

"My brother is missing," McGovern said, and ran out of the saloon.

Clint went up the stairs to search for Mandy's room. It wasn't hard to find, as the door was open and she was lying on the bed, sobbing.

"Mandy? Are you all right?"

She sat up quickly, her eyes frightened, but the fear went away when she saw him.

"Oh, Clint," she said in relief, "I thought he was going to kill me this time."

Clint saw the bruises on her face. Her dress was ripped, revealing one ripe, pale breast, and there were bruises there, too.

"That was you screaming?"

"Yes," she admitted, "but there was someone else, too. Then when we heard the shot, Frank ran out."

"Where are the others?" he asked.

"I don't know," she said. "Maybe they ran out already."

Clint doubted it. He would have seen them.

"Do you want to stay here," he asked her, "or come with me?"

"He won't let me go—"

"If you want to go," he said, cutting her off, "just get your things and come with me . . . now!"

She stared at him for a few moments, then got off the bed and started packing things into a small suitcase.

"Let's go," she said.

When they went out the door together, they came face-to-face with Hawkins and Doby.

"Where are you going, Mandy?" Doby asked.

"I'm leaving."

"Does Frank know?" Hawkins asked.

"He ran out of here," she said. "He'll know when he comes back."

"He ain't gonna like it," Doby said.

"She doesn't care whether he likes it or not," Clint said. "She's leaving. Are you men going to move aside?"

Hawkins and Doby exchanged a glance, and then they both moved. Neither wanted to die over Frank McGovern's woman.

"Take her," Hawkins said.

Clint took her.

FORTY-TWO

"Where are we going?" Mandy asked as Clint pulled her along at a run.

"The hotel."

"Why?"

"One, to get you a room," he said, "and two, to stop a bloodbath."

Frank McGovern entered the hotel and glared at the desk clerk.

"I don't know anything," the man said. "Honest. The shot came from upstairs." And he ducked down beneath the desk.

McGovern went up the stairs. When he reached the top, he found the hallway full of people.

"Come on, everyone," someone was saying, "back to your rooms. There's nothing to see."

They certainly weren't paying any attention, but then someone turned around and saw McGovern.

"Hey," he yelled, "it's Frank McGovern!"

That was all they needed. Everyone knew that the dead man was McGovern's brother. Not wanting to be caught in a hail of bullets, they all turned and ran for their rooms, slamming their doors. By the time the commotion had died down, only two doors were open, almost directly across from one another. McGovern walked down the hall.

Before Frank McGovern could enter the room, Adam grabbed the gun from the mayor and warned, "Don't anybody say a word."

McGovern came in and looked down at his fallen brother.

"Stupid," he said to the dead man. "I told you not to bother with her. I told you."

He looked around the room, looked each person in the eye.

"Who killed him?"

"I did," Adam Heath said immediately.

"He didn't have a gun," McGovern said flatly.

"He was attacking Gretchen."

"He didn't have a gun."

"He was tearing her clothes off!"

"He didn't have a goddamned gun!" McGovern shouted.

Adam stared at the man. "I'm sorry. I didn't have a choice."

McGovern stared back at Adam for a few moments. If he noticed that the sheriff had a gun in his hand and one in his holster, he didn't comment on it.

"You wanted it this way, Sheriff," he said, finally.

"What way?"

"You and me," McGovern said. "That's what you've wanted from the beginning, to show what a big man you are." He reached down, grabbed one of his brother's arms, and hauled him up onto his shoulder. Then he turned to look at Adam again.

"Well, you're gonna get what you wanted," he said. With that he turned and walked off down the hall.

"Why'd you do that?" the mayor asked.

"He would have killed you," Adam said.

"But . . . now he'll go after you."

"That's my worry," Adam said. "Are you all right?" he asked Gretchen.

"I'm fine—now."

"All of you just stay in your rooms, understand? Just stay put."

"Adam," the mayor said, "I . . . I don't know how to say—"

"Just stay in your room and keep Gretchen inside, Mayor," Adam said. "That will be thanks enough."

When Clint entered the hotel with Mandy, he saw Frank McGovern coming down the stairs, carrying his brother's body. They stopped in the middle of the lobby to eye each other. McGovern looked first at Mandy, and then at Clint, before speaking.

"You want her," he said, "you can have her, but that young sheriff? He's a dead man."

"What happened?"

"He killed my brother."

"Why?"

"Ask him," McGovern said. "I don't care why. I only know he killed him, and Virgil didn't have a gun. You can have her, and you can have the town. All I want is that punk sheriff."

"McGovern—"

"Keep my men in a cell," he went on, "I don't care, but I'm gonna have that sheriff. You wait and see."

"McGovern, go against me, not him—"

"I wouldn't draw against you in a fair fight, Adams," McGovern said. "You'd kill me. I know that. I'm not stupid. But I don't have a fight with you. I do with that sheriff. You tell him to be ready for me. You teach him if you have to, but make sure he's ready."

"For when?"

"I don't know," McGovern said. "I got to bury my

brother. I got to mourn. I'll let him know, don't worry. He'll see it coming.''

He looked at Mandy then, who cringed, but he didn't say anything. He just turned and left, not struggling at all beneath the weight of his brother's body.

FORTY-THREE

Clint got Mandy settled in a room and took care of the bill for a few days. After that, he went back to the jail to see if the prisoners were still there. He only had to take one look at Adam's face to know the answer to that.

"They're gone," Adam said.

"Must have been Hawkins and Doby," Clint said. "They saw me take Mandy out, knew something was going on at the hotel, so they came over here and let them out."

"They're at full strength again."

"And another gun arrives tomorrow," Clint said. "Only McGovern's priorities are different now."

"How's that?"

"He says we can have the town back, he only wants you," Clint explained.

"Well," Adam said, "that's half my job done if we have the town back."

"You have to explain something to me."

"What's that?"

"I need to know how you managed to shoot Virgil McGovern when you couldn't have possibly done it."

"Why not?"

"Because you had just left when I heard the shot."

163

"Maybe there was more than one shot."

"And I missed it? I don't think so. Who shot Virgil, Adam? Gretchen?"

"No!" Adam said, quickly. "Gretchen couldn't shoot anyone. It was her father."

"Why?"

"Virgil was attacking her. He had ripped her dress and was . . . pawing her. The mayor rushed in, saw what was happening, and shot him."

"But you told McGovern that you shot him. To protect the mayor?" Clint asked. "Or Gretchen's father?"

"Both."

"And now all McGovern wants is you."

"Does that mean he'll face me alone? Just him and me?" Adam asked.

"I don't know exactly what it means, Adam," Clint said. "I don't know him well; and with his brother dead, it would be hard to predict his actions even if I did know him better."

"But if he's willing to face me alone—"

"Are *you* ready to face *him*?"

"You haven't seen me draw," Adam said. "I'm pretty fast."

"Fast doesn't do it," Clint said. "Being fast doesn't kill people. Can you hit what you shoot at?"

"Yes."

"Can you draw and hit what you shoot at?"

"Yes."

"Every time?"

"Well . . . not every time . . . most of the time . . ."

"Have you ever shot another person before?"

"No."

"But you're ready to do it now?"

"Well . . . I'd rather not . . . but if I have to . . ."

Clint stepped back and faced Adam.

"Draw on me."

"What?"

"Go ahead, draw."

"I can't beat you."

"You don't have to beat me," Clint said. "I just want to see your move."

"Well, all right . . ."

Adam settled himself, then dropped his hand to his side and drew. Clint had to admit it was a pretty good move. Maybe that was another bit of evidence that Adam was actually his son, he thought.

"Well?" Adam asked, holstering his gun.

"You need schooling," Clint said. "I need to see if you can hit what you shoot at."

"I told you," Adam said, "I can hit what I aim at almost every—"

"Not what you aim at," Clint said, cutting him off, "what you shoot at—and not *almost* every time, Adam, *every* time."

"Who hits what they shoot at all the time?" Adam asked, and then added, "Besides you?"

"Plenty of men," Clint said. "It's the only way to stay alive, Adam. If you're going to count on your gun, you cannot ever miss!"

Adam frowned, considering Clint's words.

"I'm going back to the hotel," Clint said. "There's no point in staying here now."

"I'll stay here," Adam said. "I want to think."

"Think long and hard, Adam," Clint said. "If facing McGovern is what you want to do, I'll help you . . . but be sure."

"All right."

"I'll see you in the morning. Come to the hotel for breakfast."

"I will."

Clint walked to the door, repeated, "Think very hard, Adam," and left.

FORTY-FOUR

Clint went back to his hotel and reclaimed his room. He was only there long enough to remove his gun belt and boots when there was a knock on the door. He took his gun from its holster and went to answer it. When he opened it a crack, he saw Mandy standing in the hall, wearing a robe.

"Can I come in?" she asked.

"Sure," he said. He backed away to allow her to enter. She closed the door behind her, quietly.

"How did you know I was here?" he asked.

"I was looking out the window, waiting for Frank to come and get me."

"He won't," Clint said. "He's too upset about Virgil's death."

"I know," she said. "My head tells me that but my heart tells me something else. I'm frightened."

"There's no need—"

"My heart is beating so fast I can hardly breathe," she said. She grabbed his hand and pressed it to her breast. He could feel her heat through the robe—and the nub of her hard nipple.

"Feel it?" she asked.

"I feel it."

"Here," she said, moving his hand and pulling the tie at her waist, "you can feel it better this way."

She dropped the robe to the floor, revealing her naked body. She was lush with opulent curves, and he could feel the heat coming from her whole body now.

"I was just thinking," she said huskily, "since we're under the same roof, why wait?"

"Why, indeed," he said. He pulled her cushiony body to him and kissed her deeply. He slid his hands down the smooth expanse of her back until he had a hand on each ripe buttock.

"My butt is too big," she said against his lips.

"It's perfect," he said. "Here, I'll show you."

He walked her to the bed and pulled down the bedclothes so she could get in. Then he undressed while she watched, her eyes wide with delight and hunger at the sight of his erection, hard and insistent. She reached for him but he pushed her hands away.

"You first," he said. "Lie on your belly."

"That's not easy for a woman with breasts like mine," she teased, "but I'll try."

She turned over, presenting him with her butt. He ran his hands over them, then leaned over and did the same with his mouth and his tongue. He ran his tongue along the crease between her cheeks, then reached beneath her so that his hand glided over her pubic mound to rest on her belly. She groaned as he brought his hand back to her bush and probed until he found her wet center. He slid his middle finger along her moist slit, teasing her clitoris.

"Oh, God . . ." she moaned.

"See?" he said. "You have a perfect butt."

"Uhnnn," she said, "that's not my butt . . . you're touching. . . . Oooh, yessss . . ."

Abruptly, he flipped her over and settled down between her legs. Her musty smell inflamed his desire even more and he felt as if he was going to explode. He couldn't remember the last time his penis had been so swollen. He ran his hand over her belly again, and then probed her once more, this time with his tongue. The taste of her was tangy and he lapped her up until she cried out and wrapped her fingers in his hair.

"Ooooh, Clint, you're killing me. . . ." she keened.

He probed deeper with his tongue, sliding his hands beneath her now so he could cup her buttocks and lift her to allow him better access.

"Oh, God, Jesus, come up here, you bastard . . . come up here . . ."

He got to his knees, straddled her, and allowed the head of his penis to probe her ever so slightly. He rubbed it up and down her cleft until it was shiny with her fluid, and then he drove himself into her, bringing a gasp from deep in her throat.

He was in her now, and she was steamy hot. He lay on top of her, enjoying the pillowy feeling of her hips and breasts. She was a big woman and he handled her that way, slamming into her with no fear of hurting her.

"Yes, yes," she said, "harder, give it to me harder . . . oooh, yes, yes . . ."

She implored him for more and more, and he gave it to her. The bed began to leap about as they went at each other harder and harder still.

He kissed her shoulders and neck, craned his own neck so he could kiss the pale slopes of her breasts, so he could suck her nipples as he drove into her.

"The top," she said, abruptly, "please let me be on top . . ."

He obliged, and they turned over without losing a moment's contact. When she was on top he was better able to appreciate her lush breasts. He held them in his hands and suckled them while she rode him, her big butt rubbing his thighs as she moved back and forth on him instead of up and down. She just kept moving him around inside of her that way, instead of letting him slide in and out of her. He wondered if she was afraid to hurt him.

"Oooh, oh, suck on me, suck my nipples, baby, suck 'em hard . . . here I come, I'm gonna . . . ooh, bite 'em, bite them . . ." she urged him.

He bit them and suddenly she was all frenzied movement as her pleasure overtook her. She leaped about on him, made a sound that he could only describe as a "whooping" noise, and then he exploded inside of her and she bit back a scream. . . .

FORTY-FIVE

Clint woke the next morning with Mandy's warm, sexy presence next to him. She had turned out to be one of the most uninhibited women he had ever gone to bed with. She'd told him that was something Frank McGovern could never handle.

"He never wanted to do anything other than poke me in the front, and poke me from behind," she said. "Jesus, I never knew there were men like you. I never had a man *give* me so much pleasure before."

He told her she deserved it, and they had fallen asleep, only to wake up twice more during the night to make love. No, that wasn't right. What they did was not making love, it was having sex, plain and simple—only not so plain.

He lay still for a few moments and listened to her breathe. He put his hand on her hip and left it there, then started to think about Adam Heath. Son or no son, Adam could not afford to walk away from the challenge of Frank McGovern—not if he wanted to stay in the West. The young man had put himself into a position to acquire a reputation. What *kind* of reputation depended on how he handled Frank McGovern.

"Mmmm," Mandy said, stirring.

His hand was on her hip, but the sheet was separating

them. She reached out, took his hand, and moved it beneath the sheet. He touched her bare flesh, rubbed his hand over it, moved to her butt, and squeezed.

"Oooh," she said, "more . . ."

He slid his hand down so that his middle finger moved along the crease between her ample butt cheeks, and gave her more . . .

"What are you going to do today?" she asked, watching while he dressed.

"I have to prepare our young sheriff to deal with Frank," he said.

"Do you think Frank meant what he said?"

"You know him better than I do, Mandy," he said. "Does he mean it?"

"It's really weird, the way Frank felt about Virgil," she said. "Yes, I think he means it."

"Well, then, I don't know when he'll come for Adam, but I'm going to have to have him ready."

"Why do you take such interest in the sheriff?" she asked.

He looked down at her and said, "Maybe I see a little of myself in him."

He leaned over to kiss her and when their lips parted she clung to him.

"What if Frank comes for me?"

"I don't think he will," he said, "but if it makes you feel safer, stay in my room and don't go back to yours."

"All right."

He walked to his saddlebags and took out the little Colt New Line he used as a hideaway gun.

"Do you know how to use this?" he asked.

"Point and squeeze."

He was impressed. Most people thought you pointed and "pulled" the trigger.

"It'll be here," he said, placing it on the dresser, "if you need it."

"All right," she said, "I feel better already."
"I'll be back later to check on you."
"Good."
"Don't shoot me."
She laughed and said, "I'll try not to."

FORTY-SIX

"Do we have to do this?" Adam asked.

"Do you have to face Frank McGovern?"

"At this point, I don't think I have a choice."

"Then we have to do this."

They were in a clearing behind the jail, and Clint had set some empty bottles he'd gotten from the hotel kitchen up on some rocks. Then he'd walked over to the jail, awakened Adam, and dragged him out back.

"See if you can hit them."

"I can hit them."

"Hit one for me."

Adam took his gun out of his holster, sighted on a bottle, fired, and shattered it.

"Now don't hesitate," Clint said. "Draw and fire."

Adam holstered the gun, then drew and fired, shattering the bottle.

"You'd have been dead before you got a shot off with that draw."

"You didn't say to draw quickly," Adam complained. "You said draw and hit the bottle."

"Excuse me," Clint said. "I'll be more specific in the future. Now draw quickly and fire, and hit a bottle."

Adam drew quickly—he drew *very* quickly, fired . . . and missed.

"Don't say it," he said, before Clint could comment.

"Reload."

"I only fired three times."

"Reload anyway."

Clint waited while Adam ejected the spent shells and replaced them.

"Holster it."

Adam did.

"I want you to draw like that again, *point* at the bottle, and fire. Don't aim—and don't yank on the trigger. Just go easy on it."

Adam wiped his hand on his pants, flexed his fingers, then dropped his hand to his side. He took a deep breath, drew, fired quickly, and shattered the bottle.

"Yes!" he said.

"When you can do that a hundred times out of a hundred," Clint said, "you'll be ready for Frank McGovern."

"A hundred times?" Adam repeated. "I don't have that much time, Clint."

"We don't know how much time you have, Adam," Clint said. "McGovern wants to bury his brother, so I don't think he'll come for you today. Of course, I could be wrong. He might come right from the grave."

"So what do I do? Is he a fast gun?"

"He doesn't claim to be," Clint said.

"Can he hit a target a hundred out of a hundred times, do you think?"

"I don't know, Adam. But I do know one thing."

"What's that?"

"He's killed before," Clint said, "and you haven't. That means he won't hesitate at all, not in the slightest. Will you?"

"Well . . . I . . ."

"That answers the question. I can't possibly let you face him."

"I didn't say I'd hesitate," the young man argued.

"You hesitated on the *question*!" Clint snapped. "I can't let you face him."

"You can't stop me!" Adam retorted. "You haven't got the right!"

Clint opened his mouth to reply, but couldn't. Even if he acknowledged this boy as his son, he still wouldn't have the right. Adam was the sheriff—it was *his* job to face McGovern, if McGovern came for him.

Maybe that was it.

"What are you thinking?" Adam asked.

"Does it show on my face?"

"It sure does."

"Okay," Clint said, "I've got an idea. It's risky, but it might work."

"Well, let's hear it."

"What if we didn't wait for McGovern to come for you?"

FORTY-SEVEN

Frank McGovern watched as they lowered his brother into the ground in a pine box. Watching with him were Kennedy, Mead, Doby, and Hawkins.

"We burnin' this town to the ground, Frank?" Kennedy asked.

"For what they done to Virg?" Mead added.

"Shut up," McGovern said. "Virg ain't in the ground yet."

The buckboard the undertaker's men had used to bring the body out was off to one side. McGovern had refused the fancy black hearse just like he'd refused any of the undertaker's fancy boxes. Plain pine was just fine.

But suddenly they heard a noise. When they looked back in the direction of Caldwell, they saw the black hearse coming toward them.

"Somebody else get killed we didn't hear about?" Hawkins wondered out loud.

"I don't want that fancy hearse near here until Virg is covered, you hear?"

"Sure, Frank," Hawkins said. "We'll get rid of it."

He looked at Kennedy and Mead long enough for them to get the message.

"Okay," Mead finally said, "we'll get the hearse."

As they walked to meet the oncoming vehicle, Kennedy complained, "Why do we have to stop the hearse?"

"Hey," Mead said. "Those guys got us out of jail last night. Least we can do is stop the damn hearse."

"Well, okay . . ." Kennedy said grudgingly.

The man driving the hearse was dressed in black, with his black hat pulled down to cover his face.

"Hey, undertaker," Mead called. "Turn that thing around and head back to town—"

He stopped short when the undertaker's head came up and they saw it was Clint Adams. Before they could move his gun was covering them.

"Just turn around and walk back to the grave real slow, boys," Clint said. "I'm going to follow you with the hearse. Either one of you makes a move for your gun and we'll be digging a hole for you."

They both turned and started walking back to the grave. They could hear the hearse behind them.

As they approached the grave, Frank McGovern looked up again and saw it.

"Sam," he said, harshly, "I *said* I didn't want that thing up here!"

"I told them . . ." Hawkins said. "I'll take care of it, Frank."

But before he could move the hearse was upon them and suddenly the driver stood up and was pointing a gun at them.

"Adams!" Hawkins said.

"Just stand easy, boys," Clint said.

"Adams," McGovern said, "I'll kill you for interrupting my brother's funeral."

"Just relax, Frank. I brought someone who wants to talk to you, but before we do that I want you boys to take your guns out and drop them into the grave."

"That's my brother's grave, Adams!"

"Stand easy, Frank," Clint said. "Don't make me kill

you. They could put you in the same hole. Boys, do as I said."

One by one, Kennedy, Mead, Doby, and then Hawkins dropped their guns into the grave. Each gun landed on the pine box with a loud thud. The two men who had been covering the body stepped aside and leaned on their shovels to watch.

"I ain't throwin' my gun in my brother's grave, Adams," McGovern spat out.

"I don't want you to, Frank," Clint said. "I want you to hold onto yours."

"Why's that?"

"Because you're going to need it," Clint said. He reached back and banged on the top of the hearse with his free hand. The door opened and a man stepped out. It was Sheriff Adam Heath.

"He's all yours, Sheriff," Clint said.

"What's going on?" McGovern asked.

"It's time, McGovern," Adam said.

"Time for what?"

"Time for you and me to do it," Adam said. "You said you wanted me. Here I am."

"I said I'd pick the time and place," McGovern said.

"Well, we don't always get what we want, do we, Frank?" Adam said. Clint had to give the boy credit. He had to be scared, but he sounded confident.

"We're going to do this now and get it over with. And when it is over, your boys are going to mount up and ride out."

"You think you're gonna take me?" McGovern asked.

"I think we're going to find out, Frank," Adam said. "Me, I can't wait. The suspense is killing me."

McGovern turned and faced Adam squarely, Virgil's grave behind him. Suddenly, Clint knew his plan was not going to work. McGovern was not going to back down, not while standing next to his brother's grave. That was Clint's mistake. They should have waited until McGovern had come down off of Boot Hill.

Jesus, he thought, *what do I do now?* There were four witnesses. If he drew and killed McGovern it would keep Adam alive, but at what cost? What would his own reputation be then? Clint was going to have to let Adam go through with this and hope that Olivia forgave him later.

And that he forgave himself.

"You killed my brother, you bastard, when he didn't have no gun."

"He was manhandling a woman, Frank," Adam said, adding, "*my* woman. You should have taught him better manners."

"I'm gonna teach you some manners, punk," McGovern said, and went for his gun.

Clint watched as Adam drew, quickly, but not too fast, and confidently fired. His bullet struck McGovern squarely in the chest before the man could clear leather. He took one step back and then toppled into his brother's grave, right on top of the box, scattering the guns that had landed there.

"That's it," Clint said to the others. "It's over. Get your horses and get out."

The four men stared at him, then looked into the grave that now held both McGovern brothers.

"You got two choices," Clint said. "Get out, or get in there with them."

Hawkins looked at Clint and the others left it to him to answer.

"We'll get out," he said, and the four unarmed men started walking down Boot Hill to town.

Adam looked up at Clint with wide eyes, still holding his gun.

"Put it away, son," he said. He turned to the grave diggers and said, "Cover them up."

FORTY-EIGHT

Clint and Adam were standing in the sheriff's office. It was hours later. Hawkins and the others had ridden out. Adam was looking down at the badge he held in his hand, which was shaking.

"I can't stop shaking," he said.

"It'll stop."

"I was scared shitless."

"You did fine."

"He wasn't going to back down," Adam said. "I could see that."

"You did fine," Clint repeated.

Adam looked at the badge again, then opened a drawer, slipped the badge in, and closed it.

"Time for me to leave," he said.

"Alone?"

"No," he said, "with Gretchen, as my wife. Her father said he'd perform the ceremony."

"Congratulations."

"Will you stay for the ceremony?"

Clint shook his head.

"I've got to go."

"I appreciate your help," Adam said, stepping around the desk. "I'd be dead if not for you."

183

"I was glad to help."

The two men shook hands, and when Clint tried to let go Adam held on.

"Are you my father?" the young man asked.

"Why do you ask that?"

"Why else would you have come here and helped me? My mother sent you, didn't she?"

Clint didn't answer.

"All those things I said about my father?" Adam said. "I didn't mean them. I'd listen to his story, if he wanted to tell it."

"I think you should talk to your mother," Clint said, as Adam released his hand. "I can't tell you the answer to that."

"Will I ever see you again?"

"I think so."

"I wish," Adam said, "no, I *hope* you are my father."

Clint, who still didn't know and wondered if he ever would, said, "Whether I am or not, I'm real proud of you, Adam. Real proud."

Watch for

FAMILY FEUD

212th in the exciting GUNSMITH series
from Jove

Coming in September!

J. R. ROBERTS
THE GUNSMITH